Cara Elizabeth Whiton-Stone

Sonnets, Songs, Laments

Cara Elizabeth Whiton-Stone

Sonnets, Songs, Laments

ISBN/EAN: 9783337181376

Printed in Europe, USA, Canada, Australia, Japan

Cover: Foto ©Andreas Hilbeck / pixelio.de

More available books at **www.hansebooks.com**

DEDICATION.

Unto the living who have known
    How restless were the wings of Song,
Whose noble lives have shaped my own,
    These flights belong.

But holy silences and calms
    Beyond Song's uttermost I give
To those who sleep with folded palms :
    My dead — who live.

CONTENTS.

SONNETS.

CONTENTS.

CONTENTS.

SONGS.

CONTENTS.

CONTENTS.

LAMENTS.

SONNETS.

When first in childhood on the silver shore
I saw the seashells in the sunlight shine,
And built them into palaces divine,
I used to dream I heard strange music pour
Through their pink arching halls, as if they bore
A message from the sea's great heart to mine.

The verses I have writ herein are sign
I hear the eternal rhythm as of yore. —
'Chance, ye who read may find some note to show
My singing faintly justified ; for every tide
That Life has swept, though fathoms deep with
          woe,
Though passionate with tears, I have defied, —
Hearing, above their waves' resistless flow,
Insurgent song that would not be denied.

JANUARY.

The world lies fair, beneath the unshadowed skies,
Clad in an ermined robe the heavens prepare :
And trees their crystal weighted splendors bear,
By the gold sunshine won to opal guise ;
The river's frozen breast transparent lies ;
And crisp and keen, of mountain tops aware,
Down from the northern peaks the northern air
Whirls o'er the sparkling snow that, drifting, flies.
The sunsets roll away in brilliant tides ;
The twilights linger in a pale green light ;
Along the emerald path the new moon glides
And searches crescent-souled some fairer height ;
And all the Winter's icy triumph hides
In January's bosom cold and white.

1

FEBRUARY.

Forests keep frost bound, and the Winter wears
Its sternest front these February days;
The snow upon the ground still frozen stays,
Although the sun, like a great king, prepares
To go forth mighty-conquering, and dares
To hurl his javelins that flash and blaze
From out the fortress of the heavens, whose ways
He daily higher traverses, and bares
His soul's desire, — the icy bonds to break.
Nor can the torrents long be held from swing
Of their o'erwhelming flow, and hills will shake
From off their rainbowed crests the wreaths that
      cling,
And from its long deep sleep the earth will wake
And feel its fluttering heart astir with Spring.

MARCH.

The troubled eyes of March flash out reply
To my mute questioning prophecies of Spring ;
For lo ! upon her yearning bosom cling
The red-gold crocuses, and snow-drops lie
Half-hidden 'neath her ermined mantle—shy
In the white joy of new awakening,
As star-soul'd trophies that the sunbeams bring,
To show the earth warm veined.   Upon the sky,
In its gray pallor, dazzling breaks of blue
Enchant the eye, and the uncovered sun,
(The gusty fitful storm-clouds climbing through,)
Shines out, triumphant that the Spring is won.
And hark ! across the heavens, lit up anew,
Birds' songs, like golden lightning, rippling run.

APRIL.

I know the Spring is here for bluebirds trill
In lofty solitudes where hide the snows ;
And earth, like a great radiant crystal, glows
In the deep sunshine beautiful and still.
And soon the color of the heavens will thrill
The flowers to waken, and in tidal flows
Of their own azure, violets will unclose,
And warm blood veins of the arbutus fill.
The dawns will plunge themselves to seas of red,
And low-hung moons lend daffodils their gold,
And suns unsheath their radiant spears o'erhead ;
And I shall watch the budding life unfold,
With a great aching longing for the dead,
Whose hands the flowers of Spring forever hold.

MAY.

The violets have come. The south winds blow,
Impatient hurrying, as in Summer's quest,
Straight from the gulf stream, and the earth's
    warm breast,
Whereon the sunshine lies and grasses grow,
Is now with the arbutus bloom aglow ;
The bees, new-waked to life, unwearying test
Their olden haunts, and hum with soft unrest
In white campanulas, that to and fro
Chime mystic tunes of shadow and of shine.
And lo ! great gusts of joy my soul o'ersweep,
And I am filled with passion so divine,
So strangely sweet, it seems as I could keep
Pace with the song of birds, and feel as mine
The unfettered pulses of the Spring that beat.

JUNE.

Dizzy with song, gay birds fan through the air
And showers of liquid music downward send ;
And daisies to the fresh young grasses lend
A silver radiance, as of June aware :
The hearts of wayside roses are laid bare,
And buttercups, that to the breezes bend,
In yellow billows with the sunshine blend,
And in its glow the leaves are glistening fair ;
On noiseless wings pale amber butterflies
Float by, and wild bees murmur to the noon
— Lingering beneath their purple canopies —
The clover's secrets in a lazy tune ;
And in the sapphire heavens incarnate lies
The matchless splendor of the matchless June.

JULY.

Behind the brazen dawn, the July sun
Lies like a circling fire, and burning through,
Melts the whole outspread heavens to blazing blue,
And shines till late-mown valleys are o'errun
With fiercest languors. Sharp-winged insects shun
The lurid atmosphere, and, lost to view,
Draw forth their tiny instruments anew,
And pipe the sultry noontides shrilly on.
The butterflies slow loitering drift away
From the wild-roses' wooing hearts, and hide
With bees that, hushed by heat, their humming
         stay,
In chalices whose dews were later dried ;
And flaming forth in tropical array,
Nasturtiums drink Midsummer undenied.

AUGUST.

The mists of morning hide the skies' deep blue,
Though wind-tossed sunflowers, gold with noon-
        tides, bear
Their shadow-hearted splendor through the air ;
And asters, glad with purple, spring anew ;
But the whole August glory cannot woo
The birds to song, and twilights pale and fair
Are darkened with the swallows sailing where
Another summer waits.   The heavy dew
Falls earlier, and whippoorwills complain
In forest deeps.   Great vivid moons arise,
Burning and fierce as passionate with pain ;
And, deep within, a sense of sadness lies ;
For, whatso'er of beauty may remain,
The soul of Summer with the swallow flies.

SONNETS.

SEPTEMBER.

The skies look sadder : Summer has gone by, —
But the late wan-faced dandelions reign ;
And gold gerardias have come back again,
And azure gentians and the primrose high.
The air still throbs with heat, and noisy fly
The gay cicadas through the rustling grain,
Grating the air, in a long-drawn refrain,
With tireless monotones of ecstasy : —
The cardinals flame.   Red clustering berries line
The leaf-illumined ways, and deeper grows
The wild grape's color, in whose prisoned wine
The blood of June, still burning, tided flows.
Summer dies not, for all that is divine
Lives in some goldener force, some fairer rose.

OCTOBER.

The wooded waysides with a royal grace
The color of the eupatoriums bear ;
The wild grapes, lending perfume to the air,
Riot in dazzle of the sun's full face ;
The hills stand calm, each in its purple place ;
And bees, late-searching 'mid the flowers, outbear
Their souls in noisy triumphing, aware
What affluence still hides in gold-lit space ;
The heavens in a blue ecstasy appear ;
And sumach fires are lit, as beacons set
Amid the solitudes for Autumn's cheer ;
The sunsets, streaming into rainbows, let
Their colors linger till the stars draw near ;
And the sweet days — in trance of violet —
Burn passionate with glory of the year.

NOVEMBER.

The golden days are past. The chill bleak skies
Brood sullen o'er the earth, and hints of dew
Lurk in the long lank grass the whole day through ;
The wailing winds in cold fierce gusts arise,
Sweeping the leafless branches into sighs.
Yet sometimes in the transient rifts of blue
A shadowy splendor shimmers forth anew,
Like the lost Summer in a ghostly guise : —
On graves of gentians, in their sleep unstirred,
The dead leaves, rustling forth their requiems,
          throng ;
And 'chance, by the fleet sunshine won, some bird
— In solitary flight delayed too long —
Above the pines is desolately heard
Startling the noontides with a pallid song.

DECEMBER.

Straight through the solemn waiting east dawns
        sweep
O'erflooding tides of rose, and great suns loom,
Like splendid flowers rushed suddenly to bloom,
And up the horizon, gorgeous-hearted, leap.
The skies, magnificent with azure, steep
The snows with their own color, nor find room,
As in the Autumn's later days, for gloom : —
For Winter holds a rapture high and deep,
Bearing the joy of centuries as its own,
Knowing its sacred claim to crowning place
In the year's triumph, since its sun first shone
Upon the Immortal Child's immortal face :
Nor can the glory ever be outgrown, —
Therefore December's wonder and its grace.

WORK.

I count more royal than a king's, the hand
Whose hardened palm, with scarring lines, gives
      sign
Of labor bravely done ; it is the brand
Of future angelhood ; and God's divine
Delay in giving is but as a chance
Most opportune, for truth's unfledged desires
To grow to fairest wings.   The soul's advance
Is surely swifter even as it aspires.
And who would shun life's toil, and idly dream,
When out of chaos countless worlds, arrayed
In marvellous beauty, came as work supreme
From the Creative hands ?   What He has made
Mainspring of his illimitable plan
Should be, and is, divinest gift to man.

I.

There was an enchanted time, dear heart, I knew
The infinite of Joy, for I had found
Love's uttermost peak, that stood all sunlight-
      crowned
In Love's domain.   Yet while so near the blue
That Heaven seemed half-revealed, sudden flashed
      through
Lightning, that on the sky's great bosom wound
Its chain of awful splendor round and round,
And the deep thunder brake and darkness grew ;
And now the cold rains fall and wild seas beat,
Perplexed to madness on the haggard shore ;
And for Joy's infinite these hot tears pour.
Yet, how know I that it would not defeat
Love's high decree if otherwise ?   Nay, sweet !
Love were not love if I should weep no more.

II.

" Somewhere, when I have traversed sphere on
     sphere,
And seen each planet-sky through thinner air
A more celestial depth of color wear,
As lit by larger suns they must appear,
I shall look up, nor need mine eyes to screen,
And watch, undazzled by the light afar,
Your face above me shining like a star,
And see that only music lies between.
Then I shall be content, for I shall know
No barriers in higher worlds can make
Our outward ways diverge ; but I shall wake
To see the love there I have missed below ; —
And since through music reached, for music's
     sake,
Whose first and last is Heaven, you will not let
     me go.

I cannot go to meet the fresh young Spring
With the same throbbing pulses as of yore,
For then I knew no grieving, and could sing,
Undreaming of lament.   The lilies wore ˙
No shadows on their whiteness, and I drew
Divinest harmonies from silence ; yet,
Through notes that were most exquisite, I grew
To consciousness of sorrow ; now I wet
The grasses with my tears, feeling a sting
In the calm days (not like youth's blissful pain),
But a strong turbulence that seems to bring
Life's sweetness and despairs all back again.
I turn away — yet still I can but see
The Spring, soft-gliding, bringing flowers to me.

DESIRE.

If I could breathe, unshadowed by lament,
A tender song whose purest notes should blend
With the impassioned music of a friend,
I should be filled with infinite content.
Weeping, I still have known how affluent
Was life ; and that love-laden hearts could bend
Almost to breaking, and Love's weight defend :
And yet to-day divinest joy has lent
A mist of exaltation, as to hide
The hills from which I cannot turn away :
Sorrow forever looms that once holds sway ;
But if, ere this sweet healing I had died,
(Looking on naked heights of suffering)
How could I half have guessed what Death
       would bring ?

JAMES FREEMAN CLARKE.

(June 8, 1888.)

Not like the cold-browed Night came Death to
    him
Who smiled on Death; but Morning, golden-
    tressed,
Wearing a crystal star upon its breast —
With lights that flashed like eyes of cherubim —
Came through the tender twilight, soft and dim,
And like an Angel, sent in angel-quest,
Swept, sun-winged, through some planet way un-
    guessed,
And bore him out beyond the horizon's rim.
What then? We cannot follow where he went,
Nor howsoe'er we strain our longing eyes
See even one ray of his new splendor lent, —
For immortals come not back from Paradise.
But him, who all his soul's strong forces spent
Building his Heaven, God's Heaven will not sur-
    prise.

TO JOHN G. WHITTIER, POET,

ON HIS BIRTHDAY.

Poet, calm standing 'neath the western skies,
Magnificent upon the crest of song,
In the full sunlight shining clear and strong,
The whole expanse of heaven that o'er thee lies
Is quick with light of unsung melodies
That to uncounted birthdays may belong : —
Reverent, I bring my tribute with the throng
That press to wish thee holy joy ; mine eyes
Full fixed on Life's great problems, made divine
In thy sun-written verse : — nor need to say,
"Poet, sing on," — music's immortal wine
Runs in thy veins, with golden rush and sway
That so impels.   Eternal youth is thine —
And thou wilt sing ; — sing Time itself away.

TO A POET IN GRIEF.

What time you smiled before the shadow came,
Feeling the summer in your pulses leap,
I saw your soul's ecstatic pinions sweep,
With mystic knowledge of the sun aflame,
Up towards its vivid heart as if to claim
Joy's fullest measure ; — now that you must weep,
I know this solemn passion, strange and deep,
Will bear you nearer to your golden aim.
For uttermost of Joy is less than Pain,
And, who wears crown thereof, is lifted so,
To kinship with the Highest, and may gain
The circling splendor 'bove the brow of woe.
Poet, weep on, for Song cannot attain
The perfect cadence but with tears that flow.

GOLDEN ROD AND ASTERS.

Ere yet the summer has gone by, behold
The golden rod is here, whose armies wear —
Slow waving in the languid August air —
Resplendent plumes, drooped tremulous with gold.
Now, too, the asters waken, gay and bold,
And starting from their starry dreams, prepare
The sunlit glory of the days to share,
And flauntingly their dazzling hearts unfold.
Oh, autumn flowers ! — Rocked on the silver stream
The odorous, pink-flushed lilies linger yet,
And still, wild-roses in the distance gleam ; —
Why, less enchanting, are ye near them set ?
Ye come too soon : I feel reproach supreme,
So short the summer, and so long regret.

A JUNE DAY.

Oh, peerless, perfect day! With violet sky
So tender-sad, and wind, soft floating, swept
From fresh-blown roses they through night have
  kept
Within their hearts imprisoned, — I do sigh
In the sweet pain of too full ecstasy
At so much beauty. Golden shadows play
Through leaves all tremulous, and the hills lie
Enwrapped in their own mist against the sky,
As heavenly joys that men from men do veil,
Lest sacredness be lost, Oh, day most fair!
Intense with tumult that doth silence wear,
You will be left when earthly glories pale,
In your eternal sweetness set apart,
One fresh, white rose, on the dead Summer's heart.

AT NIGHT.

In the pained sweetness of divine delight
I sit, nor heed the wasted moon's delay ;
Feeling as I could weep my heart away
Upon the tender, throbbing breast of night.
It is not often that I feel the might
Of aught that moves, save passionate despair : —
The tears from overflow of bliss are rare ;
Yet sometimes Love doth lift me to a height
From which, as in a dream of Heaven, I see
The gulf stream of my sorrows side by side
With a great rapture that has reached flood tide.
And then I know that it was meant for me
To kiss warm lips as one by angels led,
And love the living dearer for my dead.

EASTER.

Up to the radiant dawn I lift mine eyes
Where — conscious of the spring — a burning
    glow
Runs through the east and in the horizon low
Gathers intense : The sun full-rounded lies
On heart of heaven, and, quick with mysteries
Of that first Easter, shines as long ago
On Christ's ascent — with the same flooding flow
As when His nearing glory cleft the skies.
Oh, Vision wonderful ! The lilies wake
In the new splendor of their white array,
And blossoms to the same fair beauty break
As when Thou wentest Thine illumined way.
There is no death since death Thou didst partake.
Thou liv'st ! Thou reign'st ! It is Thine Easter
    Day.

IN WESTMINSTER ABBEY.

Deep musing through the Abbey's aisles I strayed,
Awed by the wide magnificence, to where
'Neath marble canopies, in carvings fair,
The poets, with their songless hearts, were laid.
Shakespeare, and Gray, and Milton were arrayed
Before me — and on Milton's sculptured hair
Adown the arches through the solemn air
A strange glow fell, as if the sun essayed
From light of centuries a crown to bring.
Then, like bent rainbows swept to violet
I saw, above his brow's completeness met,
An aureole e'en Handel's self might sing ;
While, towering near, the statued Muse's king
Saw God's own sevenths on Milton's forehead set.

THE FRINGED GENTIAN.

Moon-hearted lilies, that in summer beat
Upon the river's heaving breast, are dead.
But scarlet fires, by fierce suns earlier sped,
Through the nasturtium's veins run hot and fleet ;
And where the mountain's purple shadows meet —
Incarnate of the cloudless heavens o'erhead —
The gentians, overbrimmed with azure, spread
Their star-edged chalices to noontide's heat ;
For suns no more look down with torrid eyes ;
The passion of the year has burned away :
But exquisite within this wild flower lies
The whole year's affluence ! — Oh, late born, say,
Do you not wear, in empyrean dyes,
The soul of Spring, despite your bloom's delay ?

AT CHRISTMASTIDE.

If Christ should come to me in a child's guise,
As to the world so long ago he came,
All unafraid I should look up and claim
The heavenly pity of his rapt young eyes.
But should a vision of the Master rise —
His brows encircled wide with rays of flame —
Although his lips spake nor reproach nor blame,
I should fall down with agonizing sighs,
Nor to lift up my face again should dare.
Oh, soul too scant of faith! Do I not know
Who walked the earth with human woes to bear
Knows human hearts? And, 'chance, if I should
     go
And touch His garment's hem His eyes would
     wear
The Christ-Child's look — the same compassion
     show.

FAREWELL.

Farewell! It is to summer that I speak,
And not to you that made my summer dear;
You cannot go from me, although the tear
I may not kiss away upon your cheek:
An old, dull ache comes back; yet would I seek
No selfish solace that your heart might fear:
Only in passion of the waning year
After the grapes are purpled, days are bleak:
I am so used to parting that I weep
When I am happy e'en; because the line
Dividing joy from sorrow is so fine
That I can hardly tell which way to keep;
Yet Death will find more clear my soul's red wine
Because your love has poured itself to mine.

Love! you who know a soul's volcanic blaze,
Its exaltation and profound despair, —
Its restless currents whirling here and there, —
Its summers, changing to November days, —
I turn to you — as golden flower obeys
The sun's behest, — now living in the air
Of constant June ; whose wings sweep fair,
Untouched by storm, the empyrean ways.
Nor other mood is yours, than calm alone ;
To the white heights of Peace your soul has
        pressed :
Great seas upheaved, great tidal waves upthrown,
Have rocked themselves to silence in your breast ;
And from its deeps of pain your heart has grown
So infinitely strong, that it can rest.

TWO MOODS.

YESTERDAY.

From the first blush of sunrise, till the day
Sprang, purple-winged, to the full moon's embrace,
I stayed not singing : I was glad for grace
Of the impassioned sunshine, for the sway
Of silver shadows that slow drew away
And in the midnight glory dropt to place.
It seemed as if my joy could fill all space,
And in its boundlessness all earth outweigh.
It was not spring — and yet I seemed to move
Amid the flowers, and, rapt and strange, to hear
The birds' high transport, as my own to prove.
I sang and sang, for shadowless and clear,
I saw, like a near heaven, the eyes of Love.

TO-DAY.

I sing no more with rapture ; for a pall,
Ashen as mists of late November days,
Ghostly as a wet moon's encircling haze,
Holds me resistless in its sullen thrall.
With listless droop my soul's numb pinions fall,
Nor can I, soaring, traverse music's ways ;
The fires of song will not be lured to blaze :
Mute as the heavens, I know despair of Saul : —
What touch can rouse me from this frozen dream ?
Too sad for tears, e'en tears I am denied.
I feel a desolation as supreme
And chill as death.   I hear the ebbing tide
Sweep moaning back, and Night's black arrows
      seem
Plunged to my heart, in blacker night to hide.

I.

Across the sun, in threatening darkness, went
A great cloud, thunder-rim'd ; and silent, to
Their sheltering nests, the birds affrighted flew,
And the June leaves were into shivering sent ;
The soft young grasses in the meadows bent,
And the hushed, heat-charged air, more sultry
      grew,
When, suddenly a bolt of flame shot through
The insurgent sky, wherein a fire seemed pent ;
And down its darkened bosom crashed a sound,
As massed artillery had broken away ;
Then, rush of mighty waters smote the ground :
For clouds' black souls, that held the heavens in
      sway,
With passion of the lightning all unbound,
Broke forth tumultuous, nor their floods could
      stay.

II.

Poor rose, that but two yesterdays ago
Bloomed by the way so young, and fresh, and fair,
Something of your old fragrance still you bear,
With kisses of the wild rain, lying low.
The grasses have been lifted up, and blow,
Thick starred with daises, in the storm-cleared air,
And the June leaves forget their half despair,
And rock the yellow sunshine to and fro ;
The skies are even fairer than before ;
Yet with the rain your crushed leaves still are wet.
With life so sweet, can death mean, all is o'er ?
Nay, 'chance some bird, your blush remembering
   yet,
Will daily come, and to the sunrise pour
A song so glad, men will unlearn regret.

TO THE DIVINE DEAD.

Sweet ! years ago, when, 'gainst the sky's deep
      blue,
The far-off hills lay phantomed through the haze,
I stooped, the while you played in grassy ways,
And one great golden lily plucked for you.
It seemed as if the very song-birds knew
June's wild-rose heart had throbbed itself to maze
Of riotous bloom, but lovelier to my gaze
Than all the sun-enraptured flowers that grew
Was your glad face.   I took your happy hand,
And, smiling, bade you stay as glad fore'er,
Nor knew what magnitudes my words had
      spanned ;
For all Junes since I see you everywhere
With that same sweet, rapt smile I understand
Must crown you, 'mong immortals, still most fair.

A PORTRAIT.

He has the look of one of whom I dare
Not speak ; with deep, far-searching eyes,
That seem unwonderingly to recognize
Eternal truths ; as if his soul had share
In seraphs' limitless desire, and bare,
Unshadowed glory of infinities
Had set its seal on him and made him wise
Beyond his years ; with long, soft, waving hair,
(Like floating rays of summer sunshine) swept
In pure abandonment around his face,
Divine in the expression ; with the grace
Of beauty heavenly born, that will be kept,
Like that of Christ in Mary's dream of bliss ;
The child from angel known but by its kiss.

HER PORTRAIT.

What hand can paint the passionate unrest
Of the great throbbing sea, or ecstasy
Of a new dawn ? No song poured from the breast
Of a pained nightingale can ever be
Portrayed to those who have not heard ; then why
(In poet's impotence) should I aspire
To lift pale lids that brimming tears deny,
Or take from statue mad with life's desire
The veil of silence ?   I could never show
A great soul's lightning flashes of delight ;
Or thoughts wild beating that do lie too low
For fathoming : so I leave her as a white,
Pure, sweet, intangible and high Ideal
That Love will some time make divinely Real.

HER FRIEND'S PORTRAIT.

She stands upon th' uplifted heights, o'erhung
With mists that hide her from the world below;
And near the sun, but with her feet on snow,
She leaves her sweetest fantasies unsung,
Lest, in her outpoured passion, she betray
The music running riot in her soul ;
Yet in the light of recognition, whole
Pure tender harmonies are breathed away.
Through Love's mute pain she comprehends de-
      light —
Though measurement of bliss is hard to know :
Yet when the noonday sun shall melt the snow,
And mists dissolve that hide her from our sight,
Some subtle instinct tells, we shall behold
A fair white lily with a heart of gold.

TO THE MORNING STAR.
CHRISTMAS, 1888.

Oh, Star of morning, throbbing in the blue
Like some gold message from the other side,
That ages since the manger glorified
And the white rapture of the Virgin knew,
I watched you shine till dusk was reddened through
With blood of sunrise, while majestic-eyed
You lent your splendor to the luminous tide
That once great joy foretold. — Looking unto
Your silent ecstasy, behold, I wondered not
You brake to singing in that wondrous time,
Nor that exultant symphonies were caught
Back into Heaven from out the deeps of Time.
I veil my lifted eyes, struck dumb with thought,
Your light once shone upon the Face sublime.

IN MAY.

I watched the violet darkness, noiseless sent
To a vast crystal ; for like silver flame
Breaking the blue heavens through, the glad moon
      came
And o'er the slumbering hills majestic bent.
My blood ran swift : I could not sleep, for scent
Of myriad flowers.   The moonlight seemed to aim
To reach the half-oped lilies, as to claim
The whole fine rapture in their white souls pent :
Filled with a sense of beauty all divine,
Strange fancies floated through my brain : — I lay
Quaffing the spring, like some celestial wine,
Dreaming a bird that sang its heart away
Had throbbed its fire of ecstasy to mine,
— And knew myself intoxicate with May.

AN AUGUST NIGHT.

The Northern lights streamed up the dusky blue,
Above the hills, faint outlined peak on peak,
Watched by the kindred stars, that seemed to seek
A new communion, as the gold fire grew.
The August air, cooled by the falling dew,
Swept o'er the drowsy wild flowers, fair and meek,
And loitered, hushing them — as if in freak
Of perfume-laden joy — to rest anew.
And still, while to the sky my face was turned,
Throned by the glory, yet distinct in light,
The stars, like deeps of violet, swayed and burned,
And it was God himself that filled the night ;
The hills, the stars, the heavens to which I yearned
Were but the revelations of His might.

EGYPT.

Hushed by the deep-voiced hum of centuries,
Cities have lain unstirred on Egypt's breast,
Till now, its ruined temples torn from rest
In fragmentary splendors meet our eyes :
And sculptured brows, whereon the sunlight lies
— Colossal borne — hewn from Earth's deeps,
      attest
The dead's divine Ideals, in whose quest
They searched their own soul's immortalities.
Oh, Egypt! in your bosom's crypt, you hold
Not lifeless ashes of the Past alone,
But Art, that palpitates with fires untold,
Mysterious dreams, inscrutable in stone,
And dusk-hued vases, on whose sides are scroll'd
Dim, faded characters, dead Kings might own.

CHRISTMAS MORNING.

THE ETERNAL CHILD.

The whole great joy, that filled the world of old
When into far-off Bethlehem Christ was born, —
Yea ! even mightier for the centuries gone, —
Lives in our hearts to-day.   The stars still hold
Their watches, glad as when their singing roll'd
Adown the burning bosom of the morn,
Fired with the knowledge that, no more forlorn,
The human to the immortal might unfold.
Oh, Love incarnate ! 'bove thy manger low
The heavens, replete with their auroral sign,
Were scintillant with Love, — with Love that lo !
Through the eternal years shall streaming shine :
— Great waves of ecstacy our souls o'erflow
Redeemer, Saviour, King, yet Child divine.

CLYTIE.

' Neath the late summer's most enchanting skies
There grew a sunflower ; tossed in crystal air
Of early dawns, and with its great heart bare
To noonday carnivals of butterflies :
From the sun's bended heart had come the dyes
That made its amber rim so dazzling fair.
And as I watched it in the silence there
I wondered if I might not see arise, —
As if its flower-soul had its flower outgrown, —
And slow untangle from its golden maze
The youthful nymph from the Apollo flown.
Nay !   While I waited, in its petals' blaze,
Through haze of centuries, like a vision, shone
The fair sweet Clytie of Olympian days.

JULIANA HORATIA EWING.

Angel ! o'er whom the angels tender brood,
And down celestial shining stretches lead,
I wonder if you felt the immortal need
— In passion of some great creative mood —
To sun yourself, and be all understood
In God's high presence ? — If your soul was freed,
The while interpreting Love's luminous creed,
By Love itself, through gates of sapphire wooed ?
Ah ! I, who knew you not, am fain to weep
The hushing of your noble heart — and yet
Your life's sweet story ere you fell asleep
Divinest ending in yon Heaven has met ;
And to Archangel's thoughts you now can sweep,
And wear them, starry, for your coronet.

AT GRASMERE.

I stood where Wordsworth slept. The time had
    past
For nightingales to sing, or I should fain
Have listened till in some enchanting strain
They seemed to pour their longings vague and
    vast;
And plaintive rising, while my heart beat fast,
I might have heard above their silvery pain
The echo of his soul's divine refrain
Who sang himself beyond the stars at last.
The hills his Poet eyes were wont to view
Still kept majestic guard o'er him, and sent
In lines of color, where the heather grew,
Their purple messages ; — nor knew, content,
Uplifted 'bove their calm, that smiling, through
The gates of amethyst he long since went.

VENUS DE MILO.

Yes, Venus ! — There she stands, the world's
      delight ;
Nor will she smile, however I implore.
Her features shaped with noble thoughts she bore
Ere passion of her beauty dropt to white
Of cold perfection from its splendid height ;
And I in pathos of her look would pour
Straight to her veins the tides that rush and roar
Through my own heart, as her imperial right.
But Art its own divine behests fulfils,
And mute and cold, but never dead, she seems.
Nay, ofttimes — when, as hung mid daffodils,
The low sun crowns her with its dying gleams —
Her marble presence all the thin air thrills,
And " Hush ! " I whisper, " Hush ! she breathes,
      she dreams."

ST. PAUL'S CATHEDRAL.

" And here our Duke lies," so one stately said,
" In this vast crypt, this lofty-vaulted tomb."
And the dim-lit Cathedral seemed to loom,
And waves of silence, circling, to outspread,
As tender brooding o'er the immortal dead.
I turned, impressed by massive sweeps of room,
Filled with o'erarching magnitudes of gloom,
And spake : "He lies on most majestic bed."—
Then History's footsteps backward I retraced : —
I saw a warrior that to victory went;
I saw Old England with her proud heart rent,
And stone by stone of this cathedral placed,
Until in its vast bosom it embraced
Whom England mourned — and gave this monu-
ment.

THE POET SCULPTOR.

" My soul's sweet fever that runs high to rhyme
I will assuage " — the poet sculptor said,
" Giving hot life to what would else be dead,
Dreaming in calm of marble, for a time.
Strange measures haunt me, like the march sublime
Of the Immortals as they onward tread,
By God's own rushing music trumpeted ;
Strange glories pulse as from a heavenly chime.
Bring me the chisel : in this mood of mine
I feel a power within me, angel strong,
To image forth a shape so pure, so fine,
Another Poet gazing rapt and long
Will in a fire of ecstasy divine
The marble triumph of a sculptured song."

A VISION.

I dreamed in heaven's blue silences there grew
A vision to mine eyes, like music caught
To wings, and in its mystic eyes I sought
To read some message in a language new,
Some prophecy that in its passage through
The spheres' immensities it might have brought :
Lifted in dreaming on a wave of thought
That swept to tidal height, awhile I knew
The immortal ether — for a little space
Into a soul's unshadowed knowledge went.
I whispered : " Here can be for death no place,"
And saw God's smile flash o'er the firmament,
And heard a voice, down sweeps of lilies sent,
Say, " See the archangel in each vanished face."

TO MARY.

You stooped to place a rose upon my breast ;
Your cheek was near ; the rose was in eclipse ;
If you had seen my eyes you would have guessed
Why silence came when I had touched your lips.
Nor would you wonder that I turned away,
The deep, sharp pain from memory's sword to
       hide,
Knowing, however fair the summer day,
That day and night are ever side by side :
It was not youth (that has been left behind)
For which I wept, but when your lips I pressed
A shadowy feeling only half defined
Swept waves of pity surging o'er my breast —
Sweet smiling lips that never yet have said
(Pale with despair) one farewell to the dead.

Mine eyes are scanning, as with search begun,
The clouds, the sun, the sky's pathetic blue,
The moon, the stars, the far-off planets through,
Looking, with grief ineffable, for one
I cannot find.   Nor would I even shun
Night's barest, bleakest spaces, could I know
His face was veiled therein; but I should go
— As in the midnight hid a golden sun —
Straight to his heart.   Oh, love, I cry in vain!
Nor pain, however great, the spheres can sway.
Silent they sweep on their majestic way:
The sun shines out as with a proud disdain:
The heavens are dumb, nor can I, pleading, gain
The secret where my child's feet tireless stray.

SONGS.

HER SHIPS.

" Oh, ships ! " she said : " with white sails drifting
    past,
  Like stately phantoms, fading from my view,
Out on the ocean, measureless and vast,
  Hidden and lost beyond the horizon blue
  What sweeps of unknown shores are distant,
    luring you ? "

" Oh, ships ! " she said : " I cannot see your way,
  Mine eyes with mists of blinding tears are wet ;
What birds may haunt your masts, what wild winds
    sway,
  My heart cries out, with passionate regret
  For its own ships gone down — their radiant
    shores unmet."

"Sail slower, " she said : " Oh, ships ! still slower
    sail !
  Nor reach too soon the mystic, beckoning line ;

Beyond, the splendor of the sky may pale ;
 Still let the sunlight on your white sails shine,
 Flashing a hope to me, in messages divine. ''

'' No more,'' she said; '' I see the ships no more ;
 Only are left the marvellous sea and sky :
Only the pathos of the silent shore:
 Only my soul's illimitable cry
 For sweeps divinely fair, where love's white sails
  shall lie.''

IT WAS IN SPRING.

It was in Spring, when all the tides run high,
Your footsteps, keeping time with Spring's, came
      nigh ;
The April sun hung golden in the west ;
The clouds drank color from its glittering breast ;
The fitful south winds, warm with rain, blew by ;
A line of fire burned straight adown the sky ;
I saw a dove through violet flushes fly,
With snowy heaving bosom, to her nest :
          It was in Spring.

I saw afar the shining river lie,
With its new tides too swollen to deny
A rush like thousand hearts. You know the rest, —
How fast the leaves unrolled ; how, silver prest,
The willows broke to starry ecstasy :
          It was in Spring.

You know the rest.   How the May blossoms to
Their faint-traced veins   the   morning's   warm
        blood drew ;
How the sleep-giving poppies, all aflame
With wine of their own perfumes, sudden grew
Drunken with sleep, heeding nor sun nor dew ;
How June, that plunged itself to roses, flew ;
How, note by note, the golden music came :
            You know the rest.

How, hence forevermore, will bloom anew
The silver willows, smiling back to you ;
And mighty rush of your own heart will shame
The tumult of the April tides that came ;
How Spring, that reached to Heaven, may run all
        through :
            You know the rest.

I SAID TO SUMMER.

I said to Summer : " Sweet, thou art
   Like an illusive butterfly,
And losest to the flowers thy heart,
   While radiantly
Through gold-lit air, thou swift-winged fliest,
     And flower-kissed, diest.

" Thou diest — and if I could but part,
   With spirit wings, the gold-lit air,
And reach, oh late-kissed dead, thy heart —
   Lost mid the flowers somewhere —
I might, all passionately twined,
     My own heart find."

I MIGHT FORGET.

I might forget, if but the earth would stay
  Ice bound ; if waters would not break
From crystal sources, and so find their way
  The thirst of the young budding violets to slake,
       I might forget.

I might forget, if skies thin veiled in mist
  Would not o'ertriumph in their radiant blue;
If harebells, erewhile sleeping, were not kissed,
  From azure dreams, to waken as they do,
       I might forget.

If budding cornels in the forest ways
  To silver stars the sunshine would not shake,
If something did not seem to haunt the days,
  As if their very splendor sheathed an ache,
       I might forget.

If birds would not outpour the songs that burn
  Their breasts with ecstasy, each opal dawn,
When to the affluent beauty I should turn
  Amid the noisless bloom, a presence gone
      I might forget.

And yet — I would not stay the flooding blush
  That makes magnolias' opening hearts divine ;
But with hot tears, that passionately rush,
  I drink to Heaven my sorrow's unspilled wine,
      Nor can forget.

MINER JIM.

AFTER AN EXPLOSION.

So, comrades, this is death! Well, death's a friend.
You only whispered, but I heard, "Jim's done."
Life's been most dreadful tangled; here's an end,
    And I'm a lucky one,
To catch the thread without a longer fight.
I'm not afraid. The parson used to say,
" God only judged us 'cording to our light ";
I'll take my chance — perhaps He'll lead the way
And let the angels pass the time o' day.
Curious . . I've been so puzzled. When I fell
I did not feel a single bit of fear,
Though the dark mine became a glittering cell
    And heaven looked very near.
Ah! dying is not much. I always knew
Since I was but a working lad, so high,
That living was the hardest of the two.

But still — I'm feard the little chaps will cry;
They'll miss me when they watch you going by;
You see, the little chaps was mighty nice.
They loved me so ; that kept my thinking white —
And miners' grim is wholesomer than vice —
      I've tried to teach them right.
Who'll see to them? Their mother's dead, you
      know;
I used to think God had a grudge 'gainst me ;
But now — the thread has got untangled so,
I guess He knows. The little chaps will be
His care. But still I'm feard they'll cry for me.

So, breath comes shorter! Comrades, lift me
      higher.
I'm glad the parson taught me how to read ;
And once he said, "God's peace shall crown
      desire."
      I did not take much heed ;
But now it seems all written out in light —
Suffer? Oh, no! the parson's words were wise.

Something — what is it? — seems to blind my
    sight ;
I thought, a moment, that it was God's eyes.
Don't touch me.   Hush ! I rise — and rise — and
    rise.

RADIANT BIRDS ARE SINGING.

I.

Radiant birds are singing, singing
  While the dewy May departs ;
Summer, swallow-winged, is springing
  To the daisies' golden hearts ;
Comes the summer e'er so fleet,
I shall still wait summer, sweet !

II.

Silver waves are leaping, leaping
  On the ocean's dazzling breast,
And the perfumed winds are sweeping
  From the mountain's sunlit crest ;
Silver waves may singing beat,
I shall hear but sighing, sweet !

III.

When I see the passion, passion
  Of the roses break to flame,

I shall weeping, weeping fashion
  What the spring held, when it came.
I shall hear no rush of feet —
Silence will engulf me, sweet !

IV.

Hush, oh radiant birds, your singing,
  Mist clad, let the spring go by ;
Swifter than a swallow springing
  Springs my summer to the sky ;
Azure heavens mine eyes may meet,
But thou shinest higher, sweet !

GOOD NIGHT.

If I could only lay me down to rest,
Crossing my weary hands upon my breast,
And shut my troubled eyes without a fear,
Knowing that they would never open here —
How blissful it must be, both worlds in sight,
　　　　　To say my tired "Good night."

If only, from the fretting cares of Time,
To truths eternal I at once might climb,
Nor longer count the graves whereon I tread,
But in one moment be all comforted —
If such could be, what joy, in upward flight,
　　　　　To sing my tired "Good night."

I watch the sweetest flowers throughout the morn,
I look, and lo ! at noontide they are gone ;
The wings of sorrow are forever spread ;
I weep, but weeping brings not back my dead.

If God would but reveal the breaking light,
      How sweet to say " Good night."

This flooding tide of yearnings will not cease ;
I cannot reach to touch the lips of Peace ;
Nor can I gather to my sobbing heart
The white-winged angels God has set apart,
Yet haply I may find them all in sight
      After some tired " Good night."

What wonder, then, that I should long to rest,
Crossing my weary hands upon my breast ;
To shut my troubled eyes without a fear,
Knowing that they would never open here ;
To say to Earth, with Heaven alone in sight,
      My rapturous " Good night."

IF.

I.

If you should go away from me, and take
    The splendor of your eyes to some far place;
If thoughts, that from your lips inspired break,
    Were heard no more on earth, but piercing space,
And, swept like organ-music through the skies,
    Should reach, in upward way, diviner ears;
If, while I wept, angels should recognize
    The angel I was grieving, would my tears,
Dropt on your silent face, my heart's love show?
        Sweet! would you know?

II.

If I should watch the summer flowers return,
    And know your pulseless hands could never
        hold;
If cloudless sapphire arches seemed to yearn
    Downward to earth, as with some news untold;

If, when the moons were lit, you could not see
  Their rays, like strings of some ethereal lyre ;
If, lonely 'neath the stars, my soul should be
  Blazing with hot despair's consuming fire, —
Would this undying pain my heart's love show?
        Sweet ! would you know ?

III.

Ah ! let me say what you have been to me
  These golden years !   Nor can I dream a woe
More bitter than were mine, if you should be
  Lifted to glories you have pictured so.
But sometimes comes a far-off look, that seems
  As if your finer vision caught a light
Denied to me, and strange ecstatic themes
  Fill your exalted song, betokening flight : —
Could I to Heaven's high guest my heart's love
      show,
        Sweet ! would you know ?

UNCONQUERED.

With tearless eyes, I turned my face away ;
　And, "Art thou conquered ?" to my soul I said.
Up in the heavens, the full moon seemed to sway,
　As if to wrap its splendor round my dead :
　　　I saw, like a great amethyst, afar
　　　　One burning star.

No quivering motion to the pale lips came ;
　Nor moonlight glare the close-shut lids could part,
Nor thousand, nor ten thousand swords of flame
　Could bring one protest from my ashen heart :
　　　And still, like a great amethyst, afar
　　　　Burned that one star.

The scent of flowers came, agonizing sweet ;
　The sea, with summer pulsing, went its way,
Then backward on the shore soft rocked and beat,
　While in the moonlit calm my sleeper lay :
　　　And still, like a great amethyst, afar
　　　　Burned that one star.

And, " Art thou conquered, O my soul ? " I said ;
  " For still thou lovest ! " Scent of flowers swept
      by ;
And ocean, silver singing, hushed my dead ;
  And still the moon swayed golden in the sky :
      And still, like a great amethyst, afar
      Burned that one star.

" Nay, soul, thou lovest, nor art conquered yet ;
  For still thou lovest ! "   Looking up, I knew
Where God's feet led, — as if his pity let
  A shimmer of his radiant Presence through :
      And still, like a great amethyst, afar
      Burned that one star.

THE NINETEENTH CENTURY.

Mine eyes are dazzled as I turn to scan
The marvels of this Century.   Some mighty plan
Shapes the world's movements, as some law divine
Shapes harmonies.   The Past is never dumb :
Behold, some present is its golden sign,
          Its golden sun ;
       And Beauty's sacred flower
Blooms through the ages with immortal power.
       Yea, though so long since slain,
Set radiant in our midst, to-day, Greece lives again.

What miracles have not been wrought ?
Stars, men foretold, have to the heavens been
      caught
And shine in place : With fires of lightning, lo,
Unwondering, flashed from place to place, we go :
We speak to friends afar, and hear
Their voices, as by magic, answering clear :

Our souls adoring bow : One King we own,
            One King we crown and throne,
                Divine as from the Immortals brought,
Imperial, mighty ruler of this Century — Thought.
            And poets have arisen,
With deathless passion nothing could imprison,
And sung their noble lyrics to the sun,
As if, perchance, their ecstasy were won
From nightingales.   Sculptors have wrought
Their burning visions into marble till they brought
Its chill almost to warmth.   Men have dreamed
            dreams that Time,
Lifting to action, swept to deeds sublime.
            The fettered have been freed :
Outgrown and left behind, each narrow creed :
And Woman, higher than those ancient Greeks,
With heart and soul and brain that outlet seeks
In Science, Poetry, Philosophy and Art,
            Makes noble part
Of this majestic era, and has written her name
Upon this splendid Century's heart in fires of silver
            flame.

TO JULIA WARD HOWE

ON HER BIRTHDAY, MAY 27.

Bring the daffodils, gold-petaled, with the sunshine
    hid between,
Bring the lilies, moonlight-raptured, in the splen-
    dor of their sheen,
Bring the Spring's divine incarnate for this poet,
    who has seen
        "The glory of the Lord."

Let the heart of May beat quicker, that her birth-
    day in it lies ;
Let the violets spring bluer, that their bloom first
    met her eyes ;
Let the sun shine out more radiant, that its light
    could not disguise
        " The glory of the Lord."

In a strain of high rejoicing, filling tribute to the
　　day,
Let the birds sing out triumphant, as if sunrise lit
　　the way ;
She has seen beyond the sunrise, what our eyes in
　　vain essay,
　　　　　" The glory of the Lord."

In the passion of her lyric, Truth outbroke to silver
　　flame ;
And its echoes, rolling downward, to the world will
　　bear her name.
Youth will be her own forever, who has kissed the
　　lips of Fame,
　　　　　Seen " the glory of the Lord."

In that hour of revelation, God himself the poet
　　crowned ;
She has seen the chariots coming, she has heard the
　　chariots' sound ;
Let her soul's prophetic vision wrap her evermore
　　around
　　　　　With " the glory of the Lord."

A REVERIE.

Draw the curtains closely in the silent room,
Let the moon's bare splendor other ways illume,
Let the stars, ungazed on, slay the azure gloom.

In the wavering darkness leave my soul and me,
And with mystic searching, eyes in eyes may see
The empurpled stretches of Love's heaving sea.

From the earth mists lifted, flashing dream on
    dream,
Through my senses rushing, grows to light su-
    preme,
Till, in red auroras, inspirations stream.

From the cold dead levels to the mountain's peak,
That the yellow sunbeams spilled from daybreaks
    seek,
In a mood exalted I can hear God speak.

From the tragic bases, where the angels lie
Carven on the marbles, pointing to the sky,
Toward the heaven they signal, float my soul and I.

With unfettered pinions I would fain essay —
Tracking radiant plumage, finding thus the way —
In the dazzling spaces, evermore to stay.

Draw the curtains closely, and let me, tired, rest.
I have sacred knowledge hidden in my breast.
Have I seen archangels?   Let my soul attest.

SOMEWHERE.

Somewhere the summer bloom has joined the
sadder spring :
Somewhere my aching heart has lost the power to
sing.
The days go by ;
The grieving sunsets die ;
And yet I make no outward moan or cry ;
I only say,
Somewhere : —
Then turn away.

Somewhere seems so afar I cannot give it place ;
My dove, in sudden flight, seems lost in darkened
space ;
The leaves fall fast,
I hear the autumn blast ;
It was not sobbing when I heard it last ;
Yet still I say,
Somewhere : —
Then turn away.

With vain protest I seek this mystery to find;
I cannot search the skies nor fathom worlds be-
    hind :
        Nothing replies ;
      Nature is silent-wise ;
The lingering beauty and the verdure dies ;
        Yet still I say,
           Somewhere : —
      Then turn away.

Somewhere ; only a breath, and autumn, too, will
    go ;
All seasons are the same, yet through the drifting
    snow,
        I may not see
      The green earth mocking me,
I shall be left with grief and memory ;
        Yet still may say,
           Somewhere : --
      Then turn away.

If, when with tears no more, I count the seasons
       o'er
(Knowing not which of all the saddest message
       bore)
          If then love's chain
        I may take up again
Without its breaks, I have not wept in vain;
          The great unknown,
             Somewhere,
        Will be my own.

A SUMMER DAY.

I.

O birds that singing soar to heaven away !
Tell me to-day,
What soft enchantment fills the summer air
Drifting the marvellous sunshine everywhere ?
And why
The river rippling at my feet doth sigh,
While on its breast the rapturous lilies lie ?
Tell me, — for ofttimes in a day like this,
Pierced with a pain that is but affluent bliss,
I also sigh,
And dreaming, dream till the sweet day goes by.

II.

Tell me, O sky that seemest so remote,
On which no light clouds float,
If what doth seem divineness of your hue,
Is mist of heavenly azure melting through ?

Oh say,
If whispering leaves that in the sunlight play
Quiver with golden mystery of the day?
Tell me, — for ofttimes in a day like this,
Pierced with a pain that is but affluent bliss,
I, quivering, sigh,
And dreaming, dream till the sweet day goes by.

III.

Tell me, O earth! for ah! I fain would know,
What thrills me so.
The singing of the birds grows faint and far;
Sing they more softly where the angels are?
Make sign,
Ye steadfast hills that in the distance shine;
Only to live to-day seems so divine
That I could half forget my saddest years;
And yet — and yet — my soul is steeped in tears;
I can but sigh,
And dreaming, dream till the sweet day goes by.

TO ——

When I am laid away, too sound asleep
   To feel the sunshine falling on my face,
Or hear the birds that near the windows sweep,
   Singing, as if to win me from my place, —
Unstirring even, although the sky should grow
   Into its azure most intense and deep,
But rapt as with the things I seem to know,
   Yet cannot wake to tell, so sound asleep, —-
Because you love me, sweetheart, you will weep.

If, stooping then, you tender smooth my hair,
   And touch my forehead softly, as of old,
I think my lips unconsciously will wear
   A loftier smile, although so marble cold.
It will seem strange to you no more to feel
   The beating of my heart, so strong and deep,
But the new silence will, perchance, reveal
   Completion of my soul's new song, whose sweep
May reach as high as Heaven,— but you will weep.

And I — I should be grieved, although afar,
   If on my face no tender tears should fall,
If in your " heart of heart " you wore no scar
   That I should know as love, where "love is all."
Perhaps the thought is childish — let it go —
   But still it seems the angels could not keep
My soul content if those I loved below
   Could be unmoved the while I lay asleep,
   And so, because you love me, you will weep.

SHERMAN'S LAST MARCH.

FEBRUARY 14, 1891.

" Halt ! " breathed a muffled voice.

" Ensheath thy sword, lay down thine arms : —

No more the battle's bugles or alarms

Shall rouse thy lion heart.   Rejoice ! "

Yet, spite Death's mandate low,

Despite a nation's woe,

Sherman marched on —

Marched on triumphantly,

As when he led his armies to the sea —

    Marched on !

O Death ! thou could'st not stay

A hero, dauntless set upon his way

To a new planet, toward eternal peace ;

Thou could'st not touch him, save with pain's sur-

    cease ;

    For while thou spakest, even,

Sherman marched on — to Heaven.

Where, then, thy sting, O Death? since he
Has heard God's roll call; where thy victory,
O grave? since he has made reply :
       Can Sherman die?
Nay; glory-girded, one more battle won,
       He has marched on.

Choke back your sobs, O men !
He has outstripped the sun — what then?
The spring that cometh soon, will let
Her gently falling tear-drops wet
       His new made grave.

Nature will weep, but men — men do not weep the
       brave.
Lay his sheathed sword upon his breast
After life's burning warfare ; peace is best.
Let dust to dust return, nothing can shroud
The soul of Sherman. Be not overbowed
With grief, rather let joy exalt ;
       For even Death's grim " Halt ! "

His progress could not stay ;
He saw the coming day
And 'neath the sunrise marched, as toward the sea,
Marched — marched — to immortality.

A SEASIDE SKETCH.

If I could only paint a picture, fair
As that on which I look, color the air
With golden light, and o'er it fling the haze
That gives the splendor of September days
Such tender pathos; whose blue sky should make,
Touching the blue sea, no outlined break, —
Then I should say, "Desire is answered for thy
   sake."

And I would show, with artist's lavish hand, —
Processions of the golden rod that stand
Guarding the pathways, moving to and fro
To silvery measures that the breezes blow;
And asters, purpling on the heart of day
With memories of the clouds, that lingering lay
Upon the twilight's breast, from sunsets swept
   away;
And scarlet pimpernels that dot the shore;

And birds, low darting; and the tides that pour
The fullness of their passion and lament
On the sea's heart, with beating never spent :
The pallor of the sand — the shifting light —
The tired glory creeping out of sight —
And the swift swooping wings of the dim hovering
      night.

Ah! who can wonder that I fain would weep,
Since fairest things we may not always keep ?
If, from the year's bloom, drifting to decay,
I could cut out the splendor of a day,
It were so much — and yet, so much to leave.
Earth's impotence is mighty : and the eve,
Grieving the moon's delay, doth hide me while I
      grieve.

MY LADYE'S EYES.

Fairer than the morning's blush,
 Lovelier than the noontide airs,
Sweeter than the springtime's hush,
 Is the smile my ladye wears ;
As if the enchanting light
 From some June-bent crescent's grace
Dropt a glory, soft and white,
    On my ladye's face,
     My ladye's face.

When my ladye's face I met,
 Wherefore should my heart recall
Bloom of early violet ?
 It held Springtime — that was all.
When her soft eyes looked in mine,
 Touched to tears, I turned away,
For in hers there shone divine,
    All the hope of May,
     The hope of May.

Let my ladye smile, and bear
    In her soul the springtime set,
Breathing music unaware,
    Fine as nightingale's regret ;
For a glory unconfined,
    Fairer than in crescent lies,
From the whole high heaven behind
                Lights my ladye's eyes,
                My ladye's eyes.

I PRAYED THE ETERNAL HEART.

I prayed the Eternal Heart, one marvellous night
   When the stars waked with me and sent their
      fire
Down through the violet glooms until their light
   Pulsed strong within me and a strange desire
To know their awful ecstasy was mine, —
          Give me one Song divine.

Silent and swift a mighty passion grew ;
   And thundering waters heaving brake apart,
And the cramped prison walls of thought burst
      through
   And fell to cataracts in my stormy heart.
I felt my blood in torrents poured along,
          Scarlet and hot with Song.

Quick throbbed the scintillating summer heats
   Upon the sky's great brow, whereon still lay
The illumined stars ; and, as if soul of Keats

Beckoned from each, my song lit up the way.
The whole gold score amid the planets shone, —
      God-written, yet my own.

Magnificent, above my pulses' roar,
    I heard the silence rushed to music's height,
And felt my spirit all untrammeled soar,
    Caught to the blazing melody in sight:
I prayed the Eternal Heart one Song divine,
      And the stars' Song — was mine.

ROBERT BROWNING.

Nay, Death! here's your master, — from his
    crowded heart and brain
There was nothing you could capture, nothing but
    his pain !
All his human searches have been merged in
    truths sublime,
And his thoughts, immortal winging, broken bounds
    of time.
Here's your master ; here's our leader — leader set
    new heights to climb.

" Nobler than a warrior's glory he has won," we
    say.
He has led the world's great chorus in its high
    array ;
From the passion and the discord, from the jar
    and fret,

With his king's brow, song-encircled, chorus new
    has met.
Here's your master ; here's our leader, with his
    seven-rayed coronet.

What to him are now earth's grandeurs ? In his
    new estate,
All that life gave, all that death gave, he can es-
    timate
At a saint's true value. Like a heaven-flashed
    scimetar
Sweeps his song, swift-clad in glory, through the
    spaces far.
Here's your master ; here's our leader, lifted
    kingly to a star.

ASK ME NOT WHY.

Ask me not why I turn my face away,
Nor stay to listen, e'en to sweetest singing ;
Why, to my saddened heart, the sunniest day
Seems only as if darkened shadows bringing.
　　　　Ask me not why —
　　　　It would but make you sigh.

Ask me not why the moonlight pale and fair
Seems sadder than the skies' tumultuous weeping ;
Why stars that glisten seem to mock despair,
As set to watch a little child's sound sleeping.
　　　　Ask me not why —
　　　　It would but make you sigh.

Ask me not why the sweetest summer rose
Brings keener anguish than the dead leaves' sigh-
　　　ing,
As pitiless to bloom when dear eyes close

And Love makes protest 'gainst Death's calm
 denying.
  Ask me not why —
  It would but make you sigh.

Ask me not why, for pain is consecrate ;
It would not lessen grief to tell my grieving :
And yet earth's pangs may pierce to peace most
 great,
And love denied may grow to love's receiving :
  Nay do not sigh —
  God shall make answer why,

JOHN BOYLE O'REILLY.

THE DEAD SINGER.

Call you this singer dead? This singer, who —
Bringing an angel's birthright here below —
Sent fires of living music streaming through
The pulses of the world? You do not know —
Seeing, perchance, the smiling lips so white,
Your ears too earthly dull'd to hear so far —
How exquisite the notes that traverse light
And reach the song's perfection star by star.
Hush! let the seas lament him — do not weep,
He only, singing, sang himself to sleep.

Statued to marble ecstasy he lies,
While cadences of silence round him fall:
But the freed passion of his song may rise,
And even in Heaven, the eternal heart enthrall.
Flashing among the cherubim, he wears
His thought-rayed oriflamme of song, as right.

Nor call him dead, who, winged with music, bears
An anthemed rapture to the Infinite.
Hush ! let the seas lament him — do not weep,
He only, singing, sang himself to sleep.

DANTE TO BEATRICE.

Behold the God of song
Has sent the lightning of his music down ;
And the fork'd flames leap passionate and strong
Across my heart, — yea, burning, leap along ;
Nor fiery scars I shun, lest in dead seas I drown.

From out my youthful ease,
I have arisen ; I am content no more
With my own breath, nor can my soul appease
With wine, wherein I see the unfiltered lees ;
Nought but the blood of song henceforward will I
pour.

And thou, sweet angel, thou
May'st teach me, by the calm within thine eyes,
To bear the splendor of thine iris'd brow,
Till, flooded, at thy virgin side I bow,
Climbing by my own scars into thy paradise.

TO A BLUEBIRD.

Sweep from the south, O bird with azure wings,
That comest, breathless singing on thy way,
And bring to me the joy of other springs,
The joy of springs that held divinest things ;
      For I am sad to-day.

The pink arbutus, growing sweet and fair,
Will soon lie blooming, heart to heart with May,
And willow boughs will silver splendors wear :
Thy soul unbare, in some ungrieving air,
      For I am sad to-day.

Dimming its blue, each violet that appears
Will wear a film; and on each lilied spray
Something within its flowers will shine like tears.
Sing back the years when sunshine held no spears,
      For I am sad to-day.

And yet, O bird, if thou should'st straightway soar,
And sing to me thy most ecstatic lay,
The violets would not gladden, as of yore,
My tears would pour, my heart would cry "No
    more!"
       For I am sad to-day.

ROSES' HEARTS.

I looked into the roses' hearts, and lo !
They were not roses' hearts. They were the red
Of summer dawns and summer sunsets sped;
Their perfumes woke a song that else were dead.
    Perchance — I do not know —
    They were the glow
Of August nights, with red moons hanging low.

Perchance they but interpret stars, and so
As attar'd colors of the stars, that know
The whole magnificence of heaven, they grow
And blushing with their blissful knowledge, blow.
    Perchance — I do not know —
    They are the glow
Of August nights, with red moons hanging low.

TO ONE AFAR.

I.

The autumn days are lit
With fires of scarlet bloom, and, songless, flit
The shadowy outlined birds that southward sway ;
Moon-risen vapors slowly burn away
And leave uncovered in its matchless blue
The breast of heaven ! The winds, blown through
The gorgeous-colored leaves, bring hints divine
Of unforgotten summer, and the wine
From the grapes' purple veins is still unfreed :
But thou, sweet, knowest not.   Thou dost not heed.
I stand in shadow of my soul's eclipse —
Thou in the light of the apocalypse.

II.

The flaming orange sun
Drops countless lances from its gold o'errun
Down on the valley's grass, and wakes to sound
The crickets dreaming on the silent ground ;

The blood of June still stirs the autumn's heart,
And, as of twilight's tender gloom a part,
The whippoorwills breathe out their sweet dismays
To the far hills that guard the forest ways.
Still shines the yarrow 'mid the waysides green ;
A few late purple clover blooms are seen ;
June's joys nor autumn's pain can I forget, —
Thine is the summer, sweet ! mine the regret.
I stand in shadow of my soul's eclipse —
Thou in the light of the apocalypse.

UNSUNG.

I heard, elusive, sweeping by,
　　The song that I had sought in vain ;
But, wrapt in mystery on high,
Came through the silence of the sky
　　　　One azure strain.

I saw the Day in countless hues
　　On bosom of the Twilight die ;
Nor knew which color I should choose
Where hid the song, and so must lose
　　　　The ecstasy.

I saw the moon with dazzling rim
　　On edge of the horizon hung,
And heard the echoes faint and dim,
As if amid the seraphim
　　　　That song was sung.

Sing on, O seraphim ! Some night,
   Perchance, when I have listened long,
I shall awak'n from slumber white
And reach in an untrammelled flight
   That azure song.

MAGNOLIAS.

Twice, in one year, the white magnolias blew,
The year my golden singer went away ;
Once, when the deep-hued August flowers grew,
And   cuckoos,   through   the   twilights,   called
      " cuckoo,"
          And once — in May.

Magnolias, by the summer suns caressed,
Came back to bloom — but fairer sunshine kept
My singer unawakened, on Spring's breast ;
Nor cuckoos' twilight call could stir his rest,
          So sound he slept.

JUST FOR ONE HOUR.

Just for one hour, if I could be a rose,
   With exquisite impassioned power of blowing,
My soul might find expression for its woes, —
   Its agony of love in sweetness showing, —
And I should know of life all that is worth the
     knowing.

Just for one hour, if it could be no more,
   To wear the bloom unshadowed by denying ;
Then I should be content my soul to pour,
   Divinely living while divinely dying, —
Then I should know of life something beyond its
     sighing.

BEAT, BEAT, MY SOUL!

Beat, beat, my soul, beyond the day's flush'd rim,
On golden tides of music borne along,
Into the twilight, passionate and dim,
Where, far-off, lie the mystic shores of song.
Beat, beat, my soul!

Beat, beat, until the dusky shadows lend
Their color to the waves, pulsed to and fro,
Till from the violet deeps that brooding bend,
The splendid stars are set in deeps below.
Beat! beat, my soul!

Beat, to the silvery rush of a refrain
On harmonies that modulate and sway,
Till the moon's slender arc is lit again
And the blue darks of silence roll away.
Beat, beat, my soul!

Beat, stormy-winged, until the full sea shakes
 Its music-heaving breast to billows strong,
Till a great tidal wave outbursts and breaks
 And lifts you singing to the shores of song.
  Beat, beat, my soul!

SERENADE.

Here's the golden wonder,
  Crowning summer days,
Full moon shining yonder,
  In a sea-green haze;
Floods of splendor falling
  Passionate and still;
Here's the low, soft calling
  Of the whippoorwill.
    'Neath the bloom and shine, love,
    Sleep with dreams divine, love!
    All my heart is thine, love,
      Sleep! sleep on!

Here's the lake a-shimmer,
　　Light o'erleaping gloom ;
June's heart all a-glimmer,
　　Palpitating bloom ;
Flower, all June's surpassing !
　　Wild-rose, fairest blown !
Here's a soul's joy, massing,
　　To a rainbow grown.
　　　　'Neath the bloom and shine, love,
　　　　Sleep with dreams divine, love !
　　　　All my heart is thine, love,
　　　　　　Sleep ! sleep on !

LAVENDER.

Within her hand a faded leaf she pressed,
While sunset hues were lingering in the west;
And all the silence of the later gloom
Was haunted with the Lavender's perfume:
I could not answer which was sweeter, — Death,
    or bloom.

The hand I kissed: the leaf I could not take.
I thought, bruised hearts may sing, and singing
    break;
And yet the song remains, as dust of leaf:
The perfume of a life may be its grief;
And bliss its early flower, though blooming time
    is brief.

Ah! sad, sweet Lavender! I dare not say
What subtle meanings odors can convey :
Most fitting it would seem, that yours should blend
With living memories ; lingering to the end
In the deserted drawers of some dear, vanished
       friend.

SONG.

Soul ! Why this infinite dismay ?
On life's insurgent bosom tost,
I knew its joy — I pay the cost.
    Night drifts away,
    Heaven holds the day, —
    All is not lost.

Soul! thou art not a coward then ?
My scorn mounts high. — Nay, I repent
Not one wild heart-beat I have spent.
    Love is not vain,
    Song is not slain, —
    Soul! be content.

JAMES RUSSELL LOWELL.

AUGUST 12, 1891.

The Poet sleeps ; no more he dreameth dreams
Beneath the glittering stars, — to wake and tell.
No more he, clarion-voiced, will sing away
Men's heavy burdens and with mighty minstrelsy
Smite, note by note, their fetters free.
Ah ! what divine and wondrous themes
Are his to choose, whose feet now stray
In heavenly fields ; who, living, loved so well
The flowers that hidden in the wild woods dwell,
That every tender grace they wore
He set in some sweet song to bloom forevermore !

The Poet sleeps.   His was no wearied flight
That circled upward to the infinite : —
And yet, deep-hidden, his heart wore scars
That shone to heaven like stars.
How deep and wonderful the peace
He weareth now !   Death with its high release

Has brought him sweep
Of the illimitable harmonies.
So — let him sleep ;
New visions and new flowers he sees,
And unastonished hears
Sublime immensities of song outlyrick'd by the
        spheres.

O silent Poet ! in thy hushed heart lies
Knowledge of unencompassed mysteries.
Thou sleepest well ; and yet — our eyes are wet.
If thy mute lips could breathe the world's regret,
Then fit the song. Elsewhere thy soul has found
Music ineffable, and so been crowned
With cadences celestial ; thou art
Of the Eternal Symphony a part,
    And 'neath thine eyes
In the white light of heaven eternal beauty lies.

HINGHAM CEMETERY.

MEMORIAL DAY.

It is not flowers in any garden grown
That I would pluck, however fair their grace,
To lay — where for so long the sun has shone —
   On my child's resting-place ; —
For roses with their reddest hearts, nor yet
The passion-flowers that symbolled crosses bear,
Would breathe the insurgent passion of regret
   My soul must ever wear ; —
But with supreme outreaching I would fling
The whole wild-flower rapture of the whole young
  Spring.

To-day, let azure in the skies abide,
And sunshine kiss the grasses where he lies ;
For time, nor tears, nor even Death, can hide
   The vision of his eyes.
But not for him the martial strains that surge,
And, crashing through the air, mine ears await,

As if despair, through music's pang, would urge
         Itself articulate;
But 'bove my radiant boy let bluebirds sing,
As to some sky-swept bird their songs again might
         bring.

He will not wake. — He sings in upper air,
The Spring enwraps him like another Spring,
His heart, that sent out sunshine everywhere,
         Went sunward wandering,
Nor with earth's bloom could wholly be content,
But to the unforgotten angels drew,
And, with full measure of youth's gladness, went
         The morning sunrise through:
And by his tide-watched grave unceasing rise,
As echoing my soul, the sea's lamenting sighs.

A YELLOW CHRYSANTHEMUM.

Late Autumn flower! your petals hold
 The passion of a thousand suns,
That through your veins, transfused to gold,
   In color runs.

You come when other flowers are dead,
 And songless winds your tassels sway
When from the harvest moon its red
   Has burned away.

Yet something of its fire intense,
 And heat of summer noons as well,
In your sun-hued magnificence
   Somewhere may dwell.

Oh, poet-flower! if, seeing your gold,
 I felt no rushing joy, that sped
To music, then my heart were cold,
   And song were dead.

A FANTASIE.

I cannot find the way,
   Mine eyes see nought but dark;
The music I essay
A thousand discords slay ;
   Yet something like an arc
Sometimes across the sky
   Sweeps luminous with light.
It is a fantasie —
   A vision taking flight —
        Night.

I see the dark, until
   Mine eyes are filled with dark ;
Yet even the midnights thrill ;
In purples never still
   Hides the immortal lark.
I cannot reach afar

To notes so mocking high :
The lark sings to a star.
It is a fantasie —
A rapture taking flight —
Night.

WHAT IS A ROSE?

I.

What is a rose ?   Dear, turn your head away,
And I will kiss you answer in good-by.
It is the grief a poet cannot say ;
A sweet, sad glory, too divine to stay ;
It is an unshed tear for love's delay,
That burns the heart the while the eyes are dry ;
Something between a rapture and a sigh :
   It is — good-by.

What is a rose ?   Dear, if I saw your eyes,
I might not kiss you answer in good-by.
It is a dream within a dream, that lies
Blushing with sweetness of love's harmonies ;
It in an angel in a crimson guise ;
A golden-hearted, burning mystery ;
Something between a rapture and a sigh :
   It is — good-by.

II.

What is a rose ?   A rose is not a rose :
It is a soul wherein deep mysteries reign ;
It is a waning moon's regret ; a pain ;
A song transfixed, that into perfume goes,
Telling the all of Love in language that Love knows.

Some wondrous current through its being flows ;
It is the dead year's passion — crimson taught ;
It is a dazzling fantasy ; a thought
That, where it touched the fire of sunrise, shows
A poet's exaltation attar'd to a rose.

DREAMS.

I would not cut your youthful dreams adrift
  From youth that gave them glow,
But let life's deeper waters swell and lift
    Diviner dreams that grow.
      Dreams may go by ;
    But dreams, — dreams cannot die.

Youth's fairest aspirations are but base
  To fairest work begun :
Climb, dream by dream, till to the statue's face,
    The immortal grace is won.
      Dreams may go by ;
    But dreams, — dreams cannot die.

JULIA ROMANA ANAGNOS.

She waked to Rome : —
Its seven majestic hills that towered away
Her cradle sentinelled ; and from the dome
Of its great vast cathedral, day by day
The longing sunshine dropt, till at her feet it lay.

Her spirit drew
From the charmed atmosphere an unshaped lyre ;
And the old stately Roman grandeurs grew
Into her senses as a rose drinks fire
From splendid summer suns, unconscious of desire.

Like the sky's blue,
With depths unsearchable, she went her ways ;
The wondering world drew near, while flashing
        through
Her simple words, came sparks of lyric's blaze,
Lighted in golden dreams of the old classic days.

Higher than are
The smiles on Rome's unbreathing statues' lips
The look she wore, but like some tender star
That in its occultation shining slips
Behind some larger light, Heaven drew her to
    eclipse.

And so — she sleeps,
A nightingale o'ertaken by death's dark
Before the listening skies had heard her deeps
Of unwaked music, that are rising — Hark ! —
On the skies' other side, above the rainbow's arc.

REMEMBRANCE.

It was only a little sock,
That was dropt erewhile on the floor ;
But the shape of the baby's foot it bore,
And I kiss'd it and laid it away
— It seems but the other day —
Now — my lamb is of God's own flock.

And the flood-gates of memory ope :
With his eyes, that were purple-dark,
Lighted up as with Heaven's own spark,
Seraphic, he questioned my own :
Now — the whole earth has been outgrown,
And his soul has found infinite scope.

But my heart is wearing a scar
Of a wound that went down to its root,
That has shape like a tiny foot.
This is all — to my mortal sight —
But an angel sandalled with light
Is rising from star to star.

TO HELEN IN HEAVEN.

I gave you, on one golden summer's day,
A rose, — because I knew you fair and sweet ;
Now that the skies have lured your heart away,
   Let roses unplucked stay :
I cannot reach to lay them at your feet.

And since your wings have crossed the dazzling
  line,
I wonder how I dared your lips to kiss :
But when in Heaven you pluck a rose divine,
   Wear it, O saint ! as sign
That deathless love is part of heavenly bliss.

I SIT BESIDE MY DEAD.

I sit beside my dead,
Silent, and cold, and infinitely dear, —
    With passion of my grief uncomforted,
    Watching the autumn moon that rises red,
Without one grieving moan, one falling tear.

    Others I loved have slept,
Smiling themselves to heaven with lips divine ;
    But then with flooding tenderness I wept
    I knew that all Love's holiest I kept ;
That, though their hearts were stilled, the
        dead I kissed were mine.

    But this is new despair, —
For majesty of death has been denied ;
    The bitter knowledge in my soul I bear :
    I cannot say Love waiteth otherwhere :
I sit beside my dead — my dead who has not
        died.

LAMENTS.

PRELUDE.

I have looked long, with unforgetting eyes,
Into the little children's vacant places ;
Seeing, forevermore, the visions rise
    Of their immortal faces.

And tears, that ofttimes were too hot to fall,
That might have eased, a gentle solace bringing,
From out my heart — as lightning 'scaped from
    thrall —
    Have scorched themselves to singing.

RACHAEL.

If some white angel had come down and said,
"God keeps sweet space to lay your darling's head,"
And questioned — "Which one, out of all the three
(My flock so thinned), was dearest unto me ?" —
Could I have answered, as I should to-day,
Knowing my whitest dove, though not yet flown
        away ?

Nay ! if he still had tarried, Heavenly sent,
Saying, " Although your aching heart is spent
With constant weeping, yet I fain must take
Your purest lily, for the lily's sake " —
Should I have trembling known which was most
        fair ?
Would not the one he chose have seemed most
        hard to spare ?

Ah, it is well that angels come not so !
Love has no choice but drink the dregs of woe.

If in the sacred silence of my heart
I kept an idol that was set apart,
Heaven has made claim, and I can never touch
The forehead of my boy, whose coming was so
     much.

He was my only son : he never knew
An older brother's care, though there were two,
Born years ago, with natures all too fine
For human rearing, that God made divine ;
And he no longer marvels at the tie
He scarce could understand, since they were never
     by.

Through the long, silent, summer days, I weep :
How can the lilies bloom, and he asleep ?
And memories of his life, foreshadowing
Its Heaven in sweetness, do but add a sting
To this, my crowning sorrow, and unsheath
A sharp despair, that pierces mightier than grief.

They say that " It is well ! " that " All of bliss
Is his ! " — but 'tis the living touch I miss.

And of his dawning glory not a doubt
Ever arises, — but I stand without :
It needs a higher faith than mine to see,
Although I know his peace, that " It is well " for
      me.

Ah ! many a scathing sorrow have I known ;
And so familiar has the Presence grown
That I could almost wonder, when I dare
To smile, lest weeping come in unaware ;
And yet my saddened life goes on again : —
The scabbard of the sword is seldom cut in twain.

If I one hour his little head could hold
And take the hands I can no more enfold,
Could press my lips once more upon his face,
I should be willing then to give him place
Among the angels ; but it cannot be : —
My heart has reached ebb-tide, that knew the ful-
      ler sea.

But in that Heaven of which he often spake,
The little group I miss, for him must make

Companions, that will lead him with delight,
Through "living pastures," up from "height to
      height;"
And yet, I do not think he will forget,
Although himself so blissful, how I love him yet.

My tender little boy; I dare not think
Of all his fond endearments, lest I sink
To desolation : — Was it not too much
To hope to keep him, when I knew that such
" As angels do their Father's face behold?" —
And lilies soonest white, are planted in the fold?

Ah, "they that sow in tears, in joy shall reap:"
And I, some day, all tired may fall asleep
And in one moment find my boy again, —
Learning through Christ the blessedness of pain.
God's aftermath is sweeter than the bloom,
And Heaven shall make most clear what Earth
      has veiled in gloom.

NOT THAT SONG.

Nay! not that Song! I could not bear to hear
The words he sang, from any lips less dear
      Than those that God hath stilled :
For I should feel that every pause was filled
With pulsing notes of music, all too sweet
      For human ears to meet :
      And fancy that I heard
A sweeping sound, as hush of angels stirred,
Yet know I could not see their glittering wings,
Or reach, through the thin air, to where my singer
        sings.

Not that Song, dear! Silence may heal the sore ;
My grief, that will be grief for evermore,
      Is still too fresh, too new.
I sometimes wonder what God's children do,
Through the long years that they must wait, and
        weep

Until they fall asleep :
Since I do look with sighs
On fairest things ; because my soul outcries
In anguish at the pangs that memory brings,
Seeming as it must cleave to where my singer sings.

Ah ! the pure eyes that looked with tears in mine,
Feeling the tender pathos of each line,
    Will gather tears no more.
And while I heard him sing this one song o'er,
I felt the shadow of the parting near ;
    I said "Too sweet, too dear :"
    But now, more dear, more sweet,
My panting soul does seem as it must beat
Its barriers here, and find Love's broader wings,
Then sweep, in eager flight, to where my singer
    sings.

HE CAME AS COMES THE SPRING.

He came as comes the Spring ;
A cherub, like the Virgin's, radiant-eyed,
That to your hearts the sunshine seemed to bring,
As from some kingdom fairer and more wide ;
A glory on his face, as if he knew
How near the heavenly place his feet were straying
        to.

Glad in your arms he smiled,
Leaping to song, and wondering at the stars ;
Stretching his arm out, like a very child,
Yet with an angel's power, through crystal bars
Seeming to see the illumined lilies shine,
And, while you held him close, chose playmates all
        divine.

Happy, they took his hand,
Wearing the light of peace that angels wear,
And, silent, led him to that other land,
More radiant-eyed, more beautiful than e'er.
His childish heart grew still with might of bliss :
It was not Death he knew — it was the Shep-
herd's kiss.

AN ANSWER.

Dead! Do not ask me who! I cannot tell,
Whether it was my boy, or I, that fell
          That fair, spring day;
Only he died, and smiling went away;
And I, who daily die, am never free
From this material life that fetters me;
Yet never soldier on the field has lain,
With sword-thrust in his heart, more surely slain;
Without the bliss of death, which is forgetting pain.

Nay! do not pity; for the wound is such
It will not suffer even the tenderest touch:
          Yet, to forget
Would leave a deeper scarring than regret;
And so, it may be that with surgeons' art
God only probes to heal my aching heart;
Perhaps the angels, if they stood confessed,
Would say, Love's travailing doth purchase rest;

That Heaven but makes its claim Love's owner-
        ship to test.
I set the seal of silence on his name ;
I dare not breathe it, lest this inward flame
        Escaping so
Should devastate my soul with fiercest woe ;
I cannot even dream of him, though night,
More kind than wistful day, hides me from sight ;
Then, weeping my beloved, a solemn sense
As silence thrilling with omnipotence,
Seems bringing him more near, through longings
        so intense.
How shall I know what treasures there might be
Sheathed in that silence, if my heart could see
        And grasp aright ?
How shall I know what questions infinite
Might then be cleared, if only clue most dim
Were given to solve God's parting me from him ?
Soul that dost shrink and tremble with delay,
Death doth imprison rapture: Who shall say
Rapture may not be mine, when death shall drop
        away ?

THE UNUSED TOY.

I closed a drawer, with sudden pang, to-day,
For 'neath the thing I sought there lay a toy,
Carven, and cut, and chipped, in childish way —
    Too sacred to destroy : —

A wooden hammer, that with mimic nails
Had builded tiny ships (launched forth anon),
And kept afloat with breath on snowy sails
    Till narrow shores were won.

How little then I knew those ships that went,
Slender and gay, across the shallow seas,
Were but the pastime of an angel, sent
    To teach Love's mysteries.

For, to the rapture of eternal calms,
Lifted on noiseless wings, he went away,
Bearing white lilies in his folded palms,
    Resting from childish play.

Now, sculptured on a marble's base, they show
He sleeps, unconscious of my soul's lament,
While on the Spring's warm bosom still they grow,
    Smiling as when he went.

And could he wander back to earth awhile,
Crossing the golden threshold, granted leave,
Heaven would itself be lone without his smile,
    And hush! — he, too, might grieve.

THRENODY.

There is a sadness in each summer day ;
The quivering sunshine shadows seems to wear ;
For out beyond the hills stretched far away,

  Love ! thou hast wandered, and I see
    not where :
  I do not know the summer, howsoever
    fair.

There is no gladness in the morning's red ;
The rising sun but heralds in despair ;
Weeping, I watch till slow-winged nights are
    sped.

  Love ! thou hast wandered, but I see
    not where :
  I do not know the summer, howsoever
    fair.

Fruitless my watching, love ! for thou art dead :
The birds, to waken thee, sing high in air ;
But lilies bend above thy silent head.

    Love ! thou hast wandered, but I see
     not where :
   I do not know the summer, howsoever
     fair.

ADIEU.

I walked at noontide through the waving grass,
   Where summer daisies in the west winds blew,
And saw the dragon-fly, slow winging, pass,
   And heard his sharp, sad minors dizzying
      through —
         Adieu! Adieu!

The birds, that sunrise on their bosoms bore,
   In sudden sweeps of flame above me flew,
And, as with music's passion brimming o'er,
   Dropped liquid notes that fell, with meanings
      new —
         Adieu! Adieu!

The blackberry blossoms into trembling fell,
   And clover-perfumes to their ways gave clue;
The roaming wild-bees touched a lily's bell,
   And from its silver heart, slow tolling, drew —
         Adieu! Adieu!

Nor could I, numbed with cold despair, escape
  The maddening glory of the sky's calm blue ;
But something on its breast took shadowy shape,
  And to my pain-dull'd soul smiled eyes I knew —
      Adieu ! Adieu !

Still tolled the lilies : weeping tears of blood
  Amid the flowers, Calvary I knew :
The blinding sunshine held me in its flood ;
  But — oh, my dead first-born ! — the heavens
    held you :
      Adieu ! Adieu !

LAMENT.

She could not give me back my kisses, so
   I went away to meet the falling night,
And told my desolation to the snow,
   And saw the empty nests all still and white.
        "And this is all!" I said:
"A kiss — a far-off song — and silence of the dead."

It was but yesterday that she had pressed
   My hand in hers — a rapture in her eyes;
Now she was lying, roses on her breast,
   And with new wings that swept immortal skies.
        "And this is all!" I said:
"A smile — a far-off flight — and silence of the
    dead."

Since then, the birds have built their nests anew,
And warmer air with singing has been rent ;
But song nor sighs can pierce the skies' soft blue,
And reach that other summer where she went.
Darkness has fallen instead :
And there is no reply — but silence of the dead.

LET ME BUT BE A BIRD.

Let me but be a bird with power of reaching
  The blue divineness of the skies above,
And I would sing with passion of beseeching,
    Until the heavens were rent with pain of love ;
        Then, piercing through to mine,
I might hear answering notes of song divine.

Ah ! what delight, no inward barriers heeding,
  Defying weariness to hold in place,
One swift, electric flash of thought but needing
    To sweep my soul through sunrise flames of space ;
        Then, seeing the heavens apart,
I might float through, dear love, and find thy heart.

HIS SIXTH BIRTHDAY.

He would be six to-day ;
My brave, blithe boy : and I have learned to say,
" He would have been," and not, " He is."
Yet, pierced with sweetest memories,
I cannot bear to lift my head awhile,
To meet the coming Spring's returning smile.
Other than sunshine now doth blind my eyes ;
I cannot watch it woo the willing skies :
Rather the wintry tempests that have swept
To desolation, weeping while I wept.
Nay ! when the birds do sing, as if forgetting
The tidal wave of my last year's regretting,
Their unchanged rapture seems to wake
The same tumultuous throes as when my heart did
break.

Yet, from thine eyes, O Spring !
I cannot wholly turn, since thou did'st bring

This overflowing cup of joy —
>The birthday of my absent boy.
I called thee fair ; then cruel, though still fair,
With the same hand thou gavest me despair :
Giving and taking — with just five years' space
For blind, blind worship, — then the empty place.
And yet the gentler May did bring the blow
That left my boy his blissful way to go,
And me to death. If death could still grief's
>passion, —
If only angels some sweet way could fashion
>To linger near us when we weep, —
It would not be so hard to let the children sleep.

>Ah ! who will take my place,
And kiss him softly on his upturned face
With kisses, one for every year,
>Just as I always used to here ?
It is the first birthday he ever spent
Away from me ; no wonder I am rent
With grievous weeping : yet I know that he
Doth walk with Christ, and Christ doth pity me.

Child of my inmost depths, take from my soul,
Outreaching after thee, the Eternal whole
Of love! I cannot see his heavenly growing,
But Sharon's roses are forever blowing;
    And what did seem his life's eclipse
Was but Death's shadow lifting him to the Eternal
    lips.

HIS SEVENTH BIRTHDAY.

He cannot come to-day,
And lean his loving head upon my breast,
Bringing me back such blissful sense of rest,
Or look at me with the old, tender smile
That I have missed for such a dreary while.
I cannot tell my boy how he has grown
Since the last year I held him for my own ;
But angels may keep festival in Heaven
      That he is seven
        To-day.

      I should not be so sad
If I could bid my selfish longings fly ;
His joy would be enough to satisfy.
But I am weak ; I cannot still the pain,
Knowing that I shall reach my arms in vain,
Because he is away.　My heart is worn
All threadbare with regrettings it has borne.
Ah ! can he hear me say, dwelling in Heaven,
      " Sweet, thou art seven
        To-day " ?

Never but five to me !
With him afar, the birthdays that are past
Do seem as naught, only as landmarks vast
Set in my heart's great wilderness of woe.
And yet it would be sweet if I could know
How angelhood doth glorify, how bliss
Transfigures ; but I might not dare to kiss
His brow, or say, flooded with light of Heaven,
     " Sweet, thou art seven
       To-day."

     And, if his eyes can see
The infinite horizon that doth sweep
Into celestial space, why should I weep ?
I think there will be kept for me a place
Beside him.   He would miss his mother's face
In the eternal years to come.   And I
Some day may go to him all rapturously,
And say, with love that shall be made divine,
     " Sweet, thou art mine
       To-day."

HIS EIGHTH BIRTHDAY.

Faithful th' untired spring has brought again
The birthday of my dead ; and, darting low,
The birds with whirr of wings sweep to and fro,
Singing with the same ecstasy as when
Upon my heart this avalanche of pain
In awful silence had not fallen. Oh !
Tears have been token, since three years ago,
How infinite love's grieving, and how vain.
Yet if the angels smile on him to-day
(All tenderer for the knowledge he is eight),
If lilies whiten in his rapturous way,
What is it, then, that I am desolate ?
I think (perchance as crown to heavenly bliss)
That Christ will give my boy his birthday kiss.

HIS NINTH BIRTHDAY.

O birds ! that cleave the pallid mists of spring,
The skies' clear azure making glad your way,
Stay your full transport as you turn to sing !
For unchecked song my grieving heart would slay :
     My little child is dead ;
       Sing softly, birds, to-day !

The earth had waked to bloom when first I knew
His pure, soft presence ; on my heart he lay,
Bringing great peace, as God's white angels do, —
A dream of Heaven that Heaven has borne away.
     Wild flowers have come again ;
       Sing softly, birds, to-day !

The springtime is too beautiful to bear :
In the warm sunshine, every separate ray
Sharp pierces me, as with a new despair ;
The fair, sweet violets seem unplucked to stay,
     Waiting for childish hands ;
       Sing softly, birds, to-day !

Yet Love's strong flood, grown infinite with tears,
May, surging onward in resistless way,
Sweep up to Heaven the anguish of these years,
And in its might the eternal gateways sway :
   Peace may be mine at last ;
    Sing softly, birds, to-day !

HIS TENTH BIRTHDAY.

The snowdrops have come back to early spring,
Lifting their shy sweet faces to the sun,
And with their marvellous faint perfumes bring
A passionate remembrance of one
      Who has gone far away, —
The little fair-haired child who would be ten to-day.

The great sad moon watched with me through the
      night,
While I was weeping that I could not know,
When the white dawn should come, the pure delight
Of pillowing his dear head where, long ago,
      In boyish grace he lay, —
The little fair-haired child who would be ten to-day.

Upon the distant hill-tops lies the snow,
All shining white, 'bove which, on daring wing,
The birds sweep high, and in the sunny glow,
Seeing the spring swift gliding, sing,
        Wondering one flower's delay, —
The little fair-haired child who would be ten to-day.

What can the spring bring back to me but rain ?
I cannot 'neath its soft blue skies forget.
The crocuses that flame bring fires of pain,
That, leaping, burn my heart with fierce regret ;
        The snowdrops will not stay, —
Lay them upon his grave, who would be ten to-day.

HIS ELEVENTH BIRTHDAY.

You came with singing of the birds, O child!
And the few springs that in mine eyes you smiled,
The brimming measure of life's joy I knew;
And each sweet birthday, as you lovelier grew,
I held you closer, seeing in your face
Something diviner than its childish grace,
Till nearer, nearer bliss your soul's wings beat,
       And then — you vanished, sweet!

And now the happy years that you have known
The angels' care outnumbering those have grown
In which your little life with mine was blent ;
But I — I have sore missed you since you went.
And yet, though grieving, still I give you joy
That you are sheltered in the fold, my boy,
And shining hosts may know in heavenly way,
       You are eleven to-day!

Oh, vanished child ! each softly budding spring,
In which the bluebirds passionately sing,
The sacrament of grief anew I take ;
And yet, because earth's pain can never shake
Your soul to such despair — I am content.
Your whole pure life in glory will be spent,
And on celestial hills, with glad young feet,
   God safely leads you, sweet !

HIS TWELFTH BIRTHDAY.

The years have onward swept ;
And radiant springs that would not be denied
Have come and gone since that last birthday, kept
Before my child, with heavenly smiling, died ;
And now, once more, sweet tumults fill the air,
As stir of growing things that break sod unaware.

Again, Earth's tears that flow
Are changed to violets (in the sunshine's gold),
That, wrapt in their own purple shadowings, grow
In the same sheltered places as of old.
Again, the birds, with untired breasts, awake,
Crowning their silences with song's divine outbreak.

The swelling buds, the grass
On the far hill-tops springing fresh and green,
And even the rifts of snow (that sunbeams pass
As if forgetting), — all again are seen ;
And the same heavens look down with unchanged
          blue,
Though they have hidden from me the fairest
          flower that grew.

Yes : spring returns the same,
Yet not the same ; for wherefore all the rest, —
The rushing life that, passionate, makes claim
To throb itself to wild flowers on Earth's breast,
The violets, birds, sunshine, or grass, — when he,
More beautiful than spring, never comes back to
          me ?

HIS THIRTEENTH BIRTHDAY.

Fast fall my tears to-day, though time has thrown
Over my bitter pain its healing mist,
And memory of my noble boy has grown
Like a sweet dream, in which ofttimes I kissed
   An angel, all my own.

Fair springs have come and gone, and bloom and
   shine
Of sunny summers, since he went away,
And I but think of him as one divine;
Yet sometimes lightnings of hot grief will play,
   Scathing this heart of mine.

For when I see the flowers come back again,
My soul is glad, until I swift recall
That with the violet eyes of spring he came,
And then despair and love and longing all
   Leap suddenly to flame.

Oh, my lost child ! you are with spring so blent,
I watch for you when it comes back to me ;
But well I know that wheresoe'er you went
You are my own, and Death as Life must be
            God's unsolved mystery.

HIS FOURTEENTH BIRTHDAY.

When tulips are aflame,
And yellow jonquils gild the edge of spring ;
When loosened torrents down the mountain swing,
Then comes a day my sacred tears to claim, —

His birthday, who once scanned
The soaring bluebird with a radiant gaze,
And watched the blossoms through the sunny days,
Until his short, sweet life seemed rainbow-spanned.

Just on the edge of spring
He strayed to heaven, — it was not far to go ;
Smiling, he saw its skies diviner glow,
And climbed, on fairer than a bluebird's wing.

And, though my tears fall fast,
I know how large yon sphere, — I am content :
Eternal rapture, through my child's soul sent,
May flood my own, and give him back at last.

HIS FIFTEENTH BIRTHDAY.

I trod with you Arcadian fields one day,
Oh, child divine ! the sunshine at our feet ;
And saw the clouds that floated far away,
On the blue breast of heaven in silence meet :
God never made a day more goldenly complete.

I watched the flaming sunset while it grew
And twilight bore a star upon its breast ;
Into mine own, your childish palms I drew,
With love too infinite to be expressed :
It seemed an angel's joy to hush you, dear, to rest.

I half forgot what tragedies were mine,
And love seemed never-ending dream of bliss ;
My soul was tuned to rapture so divine,
I had no thought for other Heaven than this :
In the whole scale of joy there was no note amiss.

No fields Arcadian have been mine to tread,
Since that fair day ; but thorny paths and steep
My feet have pressed, oh child ! and your young
       head   .
Upon my happy heart I could not keep :
For, hushed by a diviner Love, you fell asleep.

HIS TWENTY-FIRST BIRTHDAY.

Sweet, that to-day would be a child no more,
Hail ! for this golden spring thou wilt put on
The crown of manhood that thy years have won
In splendor of yon heaven !   And, raptured, o'er
Ethereal magnitudes thy soul wilt soar,
Seeing no glimpse of shadow, but the sun
Forever shining near, with rays that run
Irised around thy brow.   *Y*et I, who bore
Thee on my heart thine earliest, tenderest years,
May on this birthday only from afar
Hail thee, beloved ! Therefore fall my tears
On violets that the spring grasses star.
Child !   Man !   Archangel !   When I search the
          spheres,
My heaven will be where'er thy young smiles are.

THOU ART AN ANGEL.

Thou art an angel, dear !
Or I could never bear thy absence here :
Hushed are the lips that always spake my name
With tenderest love, that I can never claim
To still the trembling of my own ; days go ;
The laggard hours creep on, down-weighed with
     woe,
Yet, wearing into years, have brought this day,
The second time since thou didst float away,
    My own ! my own !

Thou art an angel, sweet !
Or else my heart would break, knowing, so fleet
Thy winging, that my last farewell was caught
Perchance in blaze of glory seraphs brought.
Ah ! I have wept so many, many tears
Since that dread parting that the blissful years
Of my proud ownership do only seem

As haunting sweetness of a vanished dream !
My own ! my own !

Thou art an angel, love !
If it were not for this belief the dove
Of peace were lost in distance so remote
That I could never hear one fluttering note ;
But now that God has given such high degree,
Recalling it, and that I still may be
Not less thy mother, I can sometimes soar
To resignation, holding thee the more
My heavenly own !

MOONLIGHT.

Through the gray of twilight stealing,
Shadowy outlined to revealing,
Like the white, ethereal phantom of a far-off sphere
    that shone,
Rose the moon, supremely tender,
And, as haunted by the splendor
Of the day's divine surrender, in a mist it hid its
    own.

One by one, serenely shining,
Swift approach of night divining,
Dropt, as from some sky above them, in a flooding
    shower of gold,
Rose the stars, with colors burning,
And the passion of their yearning,
In an ecstasy discerning, from the moon its misting
    roll'd.

Then, across the full sea's flowing,
Sprang a channel, wider growing,
Clasping with its silver shining deeps that poured
from shore ;
And with maze of glory blending,
Slender bars of light ascending,
To the white heavens over-bending, scaled the
crystal heart it bore :

And with sadness swept to weeping,
I remembered one rapt sleeping,
With the illumined moonbeams streaming like a
halo round his head,
Never, radiant wooed, to waken,
Crowned with silence never shaken,
By the angels overtaken, and I — grieving by the
dead.

JAMES FREEMAN CLARKE.

JUNE 8, 1888.

Beeches are bowed with royal gloom ;
Round fresh young ferns soft shadows play ;
Bending with wealth of violet bloom
　　The wild geraniums sway ;
Like attar'd sunshine, lit to wings,
The butterflies gay haunt the air, —
Thin phantoms of celestial things
　　Light floating everywhere.
" The world is passing fair," I say, —
　　" But oh for yesterday ! "

The clustering barberry blossoms swing
To rhythmic flow of breezes soft,
And from their amber petals fling
　　Their perfumed souls aloft.
The birds sing mad'ningly in flight ;
The heavens are all ablaze with blue ;

The sun throbs — passionate with light —
    Like June's heart beating through.
" The world is passing fair " I say, —
    " But oh for yesterday ! "

Yes : summer, all too fair, is here !
And to mine eyes the hot tears start ;
For one, divine as June, and dear,
    Lies dead, — on June's warm heart.
Oh, fitting that his poet head
Here rest, with thoughts immortal given,
And that his saintly soul be led
    Through bloom of June to Heaven !
" The world is fair, too fair," I say, —
    " And oh for yesterday ! "

MEMORIAL DAY, 1885.

It is not hero's grave where I would lay
The pure white lilies I have plucked to-day
      With scalding tears ;
But grave of one who died in boyish years ;
Who to a noble manhood might have grown,
And foremost in the ranks of glory shone,
And brave as bravest soldier might have lain,
After the heat and smoke of battle, slain
      As Christ for brother men ;
      Yet even then,
Grown to a higher faith, I might have borne the
    pain.

But that my little child went out alone
Into the great and infinite unknown,
      Seems hard to bear —
While strains of martial music rent the air.
Four years to-day, I saw the soft eyes close

With white despair ; yet even in repose
His soul seemed listening, and the notes that fell
Froze into silence of divine farewell ;
   Out of foreknowledge deep
   (Too fair to keep),
Before his feet were tired, " God gave my darling
  sleep."

Oh, mothers ! torn with passionate regrets,
The while you place your mourning violets,
   Do I not know
The graves whereon the wild flowers softly blow
Hold portions of your heaven ? For I can claim
Kinship with each of you in Sorrow's name.
Let me among your number stand, as one
Who has given up her last remaining son ;
   Only my children died
   Close by my side ;
And long, sweet years you knew I weep because
  denied.

SORROW.

You sing, " When summer comes ; " ah, love, what
    then ?
It will not bring the roses back again
        From summer's dead :
It will not come till the pale spring has shed
Its many tears, and whitened lilies lay
Folded upon the pulseless heart of May :
Then, other flowers may grow, and long days pass,
Gracing the earth with the soft, springing grass ;
Thrushes may sing, and singing, make their claim
To nests low builded ; morning flowers may flame ;
Yet summer, when it comes, will never be the same.

You sing " When summer comes ; " what then ? I
    know
The fairest summers only come and go ;
        Bliss does not last.
You cannot win me from my saddened past ;
Yet I remember when my heart upsprang,

Catching the ecstasy of birds that sang;
When the great hush, that filled expectant days,
Swept me to purest calm ; when the soft haze
Seemed sent to veil earth's throbbing joy so great,
(As rapture sometimes does itself create
A mist of sadness) when I dared to claim
A part in Nature's whole ; and autumn came; —
After one autumn, summer cannot seem the same.

Nay ! waiting bloom can never bring to grief
The old, sweet thrill : Promise that made belief.
                Doubt finds a place,
Where Death has left such bitter, bitter space.
Oh, Singer ! life seems all too sad a thing ;
I miss the lilies of the vanished spring,
And tender words that never can be said ;
I miss the roses of my summer's dead :
The subtle essence of love's past is pain ;
Yet reaching Heaven, God may distil again,
And a long summer come, that Death shall not
            profane.

RECENT TRAVEL, ETC.

Vigilante Days and Ways: The Pioneers of the Rockies. By the Hon. N. P. LANGFORD. With portraits and illustrations. 2 vols., 8vo, cloth, 911 pages, $6.00; half morocco, $10.00; full morocco, $12.50.

Remarkable for facts and for being one of the most stirringly written accounts of an otherwise unknown period of American history ever made by a Western author. It throws new light upon the section of the country of which it treats, and upon a class of men of heroic mould but humble origin, whose names now stand high in the New Great West.

Glimpses of Norseland. By HETTA M. HERVEY. Illustrated. 1 vol., 16mo, cloth, gilt top, $1.25.

The experiences of a bright American girl among the Scandinavians: crisp and suggestive; showing what to do, what to see, and what not to do.

Bermuda Guide: A description of everything on and about the Bermuda Islands, concerning which the visitor or resident may desire information, including their history, inhabitants, climate, agriculture, geology, government, military and naval establishments. By JAMES H. STARK, with Maps, Engravings and 16 Photoprints. 1 vol., 12mo, cloth, 157 pages, $2.00.

Bahama Islands: History and guide to the Bahama Islands. By J. H. STARK. With many illustrations. A companion to Bermuda Guide, 12mo, $2.00.

Boating Trips on New England Rivers. By HENRY PARKER FELLOWS. Illustrated. Square 12mo, cloth, $1.25.

This capital book, the only American work so far upon its subject, was warmly commended by the late John Boyle O'Reilly, who saw in it the beginning of an interest in our American rivers, which he, one of the most enthusiastic of boatmen, did so much to encourage and foster.

Mailed, to any address, postage paid, on receipt of price by the publisher.

J. G. CUPPLES, 250 Boylston St.,
BOSTON.

NEW FICTION.

The Chevalier of Pensieri-Vani; Together with Frequent References to the Prorege of Arcopia. By HENRY B. FULLER. Half binding, $1.25; paper, 50 cents.

The exquisite pleasure this book has given me.—CHARLES ELIOT NORTON.

A precious book. . . It tastes of genius. — JAMES RUSSELL LOWELL.

A new departure, really new. — *Literary World.*

Penelope's Web: A Novel of Italy. By OWEN INNSLY, author of "Love Poems and Sonnets." *A bit of exquisite prose (the first) from Miss Jennison, whose "Love Poems and Sonnets" went through so many editions.* 12mo, cloth, $1.50.

Stray Leaves from Newport: A Book of Fancies. By Mrs. WILLIAM LAMONT WHEELER. Illustrated. Finely printed, and most beautifully bound in tapestry, white and gold. 16mo, cloth, $1.50; paper, 50 cents. *Fourth Edition.*

By far the most popular book published upon America's aristocratic resort; written, too, by one of its leaders.

Something About Joe Cummings; or, A Son of a Squaw in Search of a Mother. 12mo, cloth, $1.50.

A rough and ready story of the New South-west; not vulgar, but strong, with a good deal of local color in it.

Eastward: or, a Buddhist Lover. By L. K. H. 12mo, cloth, $1.50.

Sure to please those who concur with SYDNEY SMITH as to the meaning of *doxy.*

Hiero-Salem: The Vision of Peace. By E. L. MASON. Illustrated. *A curious and remarkable novel, interesting to those investigating Buddhism, Theosophy and the position of woman.* Square 12mo, 508 pages, cloth, $2.00.

Fellow Travellers: A Story. By EDWARD FULLER. 12mo, 341 pages, cloth, $1.00.

A brilliantly written novel, depicting New England life, customs and manners, at the present time.

Mailed, to any address, postage paid, on receipt of price by the publisher.

J. G. CUPPLES, 250 Boylston St.,
BOSTON.

NEW POETRY.

A Poet's Last Songs. Poems by the late HENRY
BERNARD CARPENTER, with introduction by JAMES JEFFREY
ROCHE, and portrait. 16mo, unique binding, $1.50 net.

This little volume is all that remains to us of the many-
gifted man who came to Boston a few years ago, a stranger and
unheralded, and took his place among her best poets and
orators by the right divine of genius.

Letter and Spirit. By A. M. RICHARDS.

By the wife of the celebrated American artist, WILLIAM T.
RICHARDS. Psychological and devotional in character,
and taking a high rank in American poetry. Square 12mo,
unique binding, $1.50.

No common, thoughtless verse-maker could produce, in
this most difficult form of the sonnet, such thoughtful and
exalted religious sentiments. — *Phila. Press.*

Letter and Spirit is a book to be studied and treasured. —
Boston Advertiser.

An admirable command over the difficulties of the sonnet is
shown. — *Gazette*, Boston.

Margaret and the Singer's Story. By EFFIE
DOUGLASS PUTNAM. *Second Edition.* 16mo, white cloth,
$1.25.

Graceful verses in the style of Miss Proctor, by one of
the same faith : namely, a Roman Catholic.

In Divers Tones. By HERBERT WOLCOTT
BOWEN. 16mo, half yellow satin, white sides, $1.25.
" Trifles light as a feather, caught in cunning forms."

Auld Scots Ballads, edited by ROBERT FORD.
Uniform with Auld Scots Humor. 1 vol., 300 pages, 16mo,
cloth. *Net, $1.75. Nearly ready.*

*Mailed, to any address, postage paid, on receipt of price by
the publisher.*

J. G. CUPPLES, 250 Boylston St.,
BOSTON.

RECENT AMERICANA.

Paul Revere : A Biography. By ELBRIDGE HENRY GOSS.
Embellished with illustrations, comprising portraits, historical scenes, old and quaint localities, views of colonial streets and buildings, reproductions of curious and obsolete cuts, including many of Paul Revere's own caricatures and engravings, etc., etc., executed as photo-gravures, etchings, and woodcuts, many of them printed in colors.
2 vols., 8vo, cloth, $6.00 ; large paper, $10.00.

Porter's Boston. Forty full-page, and over fifty smaller illustrations, by GEORGE R. TOLMAN.   *2d edition.*
1 vol., large quarto, half sealskin, $6.00.
A few copies of the exceedingly scarce first edition can be had by direct application to the publisher, specially bound in half calf extra, for $9.00 net.

The Diary of Samuel Sewall, 1674-1729.
Edited by DR. G. E. ELLIS, W. H. WHITMORE, H. W. TORREY and JAMES RUSSELL LOWELL. With index of names, places and events. 3 vols., large 8vo. *Net*, $10.00.
This is a complete copy (printed at the University Press) of the famous diary of Chief Justice Sewall, the manuscript of which is one of the treasures of the Massachusetts Historical Society. It abounds in wit, humor and wisdom, and is *rich* in reference to names of early American families.

Acts of the Anti-Slavery Apostles. By PARKER PILLSBURY. 12mo, 503 pages, cloth. *Net*, $2.00.
An authoritative and comprehensive work by one of the original leaders in the anti-slavery movement ; not stereotyped and, as few copies remain for sale, it is certain to become an exceedingly scarce book.

Life of Admiral Sir Isaac Coffin. Baronet : His English and American Ancestors. By Thomas C. Amory. With portrait. Large 8vo. *Net*, $1.50.
An elaborate biography of one of Nantucket's most famous sons, who rose to high rank in the British navy, and afterwards founded the celebrated Coffin schools in his native island. Interesting not only to members of the Coffin family, but to genealogists.

Mailed, to any address, postage paid, on receipt of price by the publisher.

J. G. CUPPLES, 250 Boylston St.,
BOSTON.

FOR THE SEEKER AND FOR THE SORROWFUL.

The Sunny Side of Bereavement: as Illustrated in Tennyson's "In Memoriam." By REV. CHARLES E. COOLEDGE. 12mo, parchment paper, 50 cents.

For a sorrowing friend, nothing could be more appropriate, or more comforting and helpful. — ZION'S HERALD.

Whence? What? Where? By J. R. NICHOLS. *12th ed.* With portrait. 16mo, cloth, gilt top, $1.25. *Fourteenth thousand.*

The World Moves. By A LAYMAN. 16mo, cloth, $1.00.

A little book, but one that has made a mighty commotion amongst the leaders of the *different denominations.*

It has brought forth thousands of letters to the unknown author, from those who call themselves stanch and orthodox members of the fold, commending him for his plain talking and new views.

NEW VOLUMES OF HUMOR.

Aunt Nabby: Her Rambles, Her Adventures and Her Notions. By L. B. EVANS. *Second Edition.* With illustrations. 16mo, cloth, $1.00.

A capital addition to Yankee, *i. e.*, New England humor, which is steadily growing in popular favor and which promises to outstrip "Widow Bedott."

Auld Scots Humor: By ROBERT FORD. Illustrated. *Uniform with " Auld Scots Ballads."* 1 vol., 344 pages, 16mo, cloth. *Net,* $1.75. *Nearly ready.*

Mailed, to any address, postage paid, on receipt of price by the publisher.

J. G. CUPPLES, 250 Boylston St., BOSTON.

www.ingramcontent.com/pod-product-compliance
Lightning Source LLC
Chambersburg PA
CBHW020623030726
47497CB00007B/2380